STICKS AND STONES

Khargals of Duras

TAMSIN LEY

A Production of

Twin Leaf Press

Print Version

ISBN-13: 978-1-950027-08-8

INTRODUCTION

A thousand years ago, a Khargal scouting party left Duras, only to crash on a planet called Earth.

Injured and outnumbered, the stranded Khargals hid among stone effigies and observed the slow evolution of the planet's primitive inhabitants. With no means of returning to Duras, they watched from their shadowy perches and faded into legend, becoming the mythical gargoyles.

Until today. Long after any hope for rescue had died, the distress signal has finally been answered.

It's time to go home.

STICKS AND STONES

What's worse than being stalked by a gargoyle?

Falling in love with one.

After her father's illness exhausted her family fortune, Angie's made it her mission to hold onto the home that is the last piece of her heritage. But when a mysterious man makes an offer on the life-sized gargoyle in her garden, she quickly discovers her property holds more than sentimental heirlooms. Beneath its stony facade hides a world where legends are more than mythology, and ancient stories have roots from beyond the stars. The stone sentinel that's guarded her family for generations is not only alive—

He's a sexy-as-hell alien who can't leave well enough alone.

Sten's ship crashed on Earth centuries ago, and he has watched Angie's family for generations, sworn to protect his deceased friend's bloodline. He never understood what could drive a Khargal to break the Prime Directive and fall in love with a human, let alone procreate, but Angie makes Sten consider things beyond mere duty. She's resourceful, funny, and her smile is enough to melt a statue's heart.

And now she's in danger.

Unaware of her alien ancestry, Angie has no idea what's at stake. With enemies closing in, Sten is forced to break the silence he's maintained for centuries. Can he convince this stubborn human she belongs on another world? More importantly, can he convince her she belongs by his side?

Angie was up to her elbows in potting soil when a man's voice forced her to turn around. As the owner of one of Old Turnbull's historic houses, she was expected to be pleasant to tourists, even when they trespassed on what was clearly private property. She took a calming breath and pasted a smile in place. A man with salt and pepper hair and wearing an expensive business suit was running his palm along one of her life-sized gargoyle's wings.

"Can I help you, sir?" She didn't bother to brush her hands clean as she moved toward him. Tourists in the historic ghost town seemed to get more entitled every day, and while she appreciated the boost they created in the local economy, it sucked living in one of the most prominent landmarks.

"Just a moment, if you please." He didn't look at her, just moved closer to the statue, one polished shoe crushing the marigolds edging her garden bed.

The gargoyle had garnered more than its share of attention, but never as rudely as this. In the form of a perfectly sculpted man, at first glance it could be taken for a crouching Adonis with wings. But closer inspection revealed the wings to be more like a demon's than an angel's, with claws at the upper joints and tips. The figure also had small horns buried in the hair curling over his temples and a long tail tucked against the back of one leg. Angie wouldn't have been surprised if the statue's fisted hands had claws. Her father had once said it'd been guarding their family for generations. *If only it could defend itself against this creep right now.*

Scowling at the man crushing her heirloom flowers, she cleared her throat. "Sir? This is private property."

With obvious reluctance, he pulled his attention from the gargoyle and reached into his breast pocket, producing a business card. He held it out to her. "Winston York the Third, dealer in rare antiquities." As she accepted the card, his gray eyes flicked over her stained jeans and plaid button-down shirt. "I'm interested in purchasing your statue."

Without looking at the card, Angie pointed to the sign on the tall, wrought-iron fence surrounding her yard, hoping the guy would take a hint that he was unwelcome. "In case you didn't notice, this is a historic site. The statue belongs to the house."

"Then I'd like to buy the entire property." He turned his gaze to the Victorian style brick building with its covered wrap-around porch and small turret. The scrolled trim needed new paint and one of the windows on the upper level was still boarded up after a spring storm had dropped a tree against the house, but she'd been forced to funnel her limited funds into fixing the roof. Even so, it was in far better condition than the rest of Old Turnbull. Her home was no Frank Lloyd Wright, but the antiquities dealers and national historians always seemed to be knocking on her door.

York finished his perusal and arched a brow at her. "You are the owner, correct?"

That's it. She was done being polite; the ladies at the Historical Society could go jump in a lake. "I am. But I don't recall putting up a For Sale sign."

A condescending smile lifted the corners of his mouth. "Everything is for sale. How does ten percent over market value sound? I'll have an assessor here tomorrow."

Looking at York's slick suit and manicured fingernails, she was reminded of her father's stories about the mining town during the boom, when big investors had moved in to buy out all the little claims. The house was one of the few pieces of her heritage she'd managed to keep after her dad died.

Her chest grew tight thinking about her father, and she shifted her focus back to the moment. Just who did this York fellow think he was? The asshole hadn't even bothered to ask for her name.

Taking a step forward, she stood toe-to-toe with the man, eyes level with his. "This house is my home, Mr. York, not some fixer-upper for you to buy and flip. It's not for sale." She thrust the card back into his suit's breast pocket. "Now please remove yourself from my property."

His gaze dropped toward her chest. Great. If this guy turned full creepster on her, she was going to shove her garden trowel up his ass. But his focus lingered at the hollow of her throat where her mother's antique pendant hung.

She pulled her collar closed and stepped around York toward the gate, motioning for him to leave. "I have work to do, so please move along. I'm sure you'll find other things to interest you in town."

York narrowed his eyes, and her whole body tensed. She'd never been to a big city, but this was how she expected someone felt just before a mugger grabbed their stuff. Slowly, he readjusted the hem of his suit jacket. "My apologies if I've offended you, Miss—?" He stepped through the gate and paused on the cracked concrete that had once been a sidewalk, looking at her expectantly. "I'm afraid I didn't catch your name."

"You didn't ask." She pushed the gate closed, gritting her teeth against the nails-on-the-chalkboard screech. Getting the rusty hinges open again in the morning when she left for her shift at the diner was going to be interesting, but she wanted to make her point.

"Ahem, well, again, my apologies. I hope you will reconsider. I'll have my lawyer draw up papers and send them over. I'm sure you'll find my offer more than generous."

She met his gaze between the bars. "And I'm sure you'll find my refusal just as firm."

Turning on her heel, she stalked back to her pots, feeling as if her gargoyle's gaze followed her with pride.

❧

Angie lay stiff beneath the covers, unsure if the sound she'd heard was a dream or her half-stray cat, Sally, getting rowdy with the dust bunnies. She was used to the creaks and groans of the old house, and usually slept like a rock, but she could swear she'd been woken by the awful sound of her gate hinges. Exhausted from a long day in the sun, she didn't want to get out of bed to check. The sound came again. Definitely the hinges. *Ugh. Was that York guy back to fondle her gargoyle?* The statue was too heavy to steal, but if that asshole was crushing more of her flowers, she might just shoot him.

Slipping from beneath the covers, she set her bare feet onto the chilly hardwood floor and tiptoed to the open window. The honey-almond scent from the bed of heirloom night phlox wafted in on the night breeze. Her bedroom was in the turret, its leaded glass panes overlooking the garden. She sometimes liked to just sit up here and admire her flower beds and the monstrous yet strangely sexy gargoyle that dominated the foliage.

She squinted over the shadows of flowers and leaves. The moon was a mere crescent hanging low in the sky, but she knew right where to look to see her gargoyle's broad shoulders.

The space there was empty. She rubbed her eyes, pressing her nose against the glass. Where was he? The darkness must be playing tricks on her.

A creak and a thud came from downstairs. She jumped, twisting away from the window and pressing herself into the heavy damask curtain. Was someone *inside*? Turnbull had zero crime, and she'd never worried much about locking up. They didn't even have a police station, relying on the county sheriff for the few incidents that arose. If she called 911, it might be an hour or more before someone arrived.

She tiptoed to the shelf where she kept her father's old rifle. Her father'd taught her to shoot from an early age, and the gun was loaded in case a bear or mountain lion decided to come sniffing around. She hadn't fired it since she'd bought it back from the pawn shop a few years ago, and she hoped she didn't have to tonight; blood on her carpet and holes in her walls were the last thing she wanted.

Hoping to chase the intruder off, she moved down the narrow hallway to the stairwell and called, "Whoever's down there, I'm dialing 911."

Breaking glass tinkled in the parlor, and a man's voice said, "Oh, shit!"

Oh, hell no. What'd just broken? Maybe she'd rather shoot the bastard after all. She'd been buying back heirlooms as she could afford them and the few things she'd managed to acquire were precious. The sound of something heavy toppled below. "Fuck," she muttered. Clenching her teeth, she started down the stairs, not bothering with the lights. She knew every inch of this place, and right now, darkness was her friend. "You'd better leave now! I have a gun!"

She rounded the corner, heart in her throat. Against the dark backdrop of the parlor windows a huge silhouette of a man lunged toward her. Before she even thought about it, she fired, the stock slamming painfully against her shoulder and driving her backward. She'd forgotten what the kick of a rifle felt like, and the report left her ears ringing. Had she hit him? It took her a moment to reorient herself and bring the weapon back up. God, she hoped she didn't have to shoot a second time.

To her relief, the door to the porch wrenched open and whoever had been inside fled into the night.

"That's right, asshole!" She took a few steps after him but was forced to pause when her bare foot met broken pottery.

Dammit, that better not be from her curio cabinet. She backtracked and flicked on the light switch.

The sight of her ransacked parlor was sickening, but that's not what froze her in place; across the collapsed remains of her Queen Anne sofa lay her gargoyle.

And he was getting blood on her carpet.

The man lying sprawled across her parlor floor couldn't possibly be her garden statue. She had to be dreaming. Callused feet crunching unharmed over the broken China, she stepped forward for a closer look at his speckled gray skin. The facial features were the same she'd looked at since childhood, the same well-sculpted chest, abs, and limbs. But his wings were spread, not pulled close to his body, and he was no longer crouching. In fact, he was spread-eagle, exposing parts of his body that had been hidden before. Very male parts. She licked her lips. Her imagination in this dream was obviously overcompensating; he was *huge*.

Her gaze traveled from his crotch to his blood-coated chest and the flutter in her belly shifted to concern. Statues didn't bleed, but a jagged hole had appeared just below his ribs and blood spilled onto her vintage area rug even as she watched. One wing twitched, and she jumped back, breath catching. He really wasn't a statue. He was alive. But if she didn't stop the bleeding, he might not be for long.

She grabbed one of the decorative pillows lying on the floor nearby and knelt beside him. She couldn't remember the last time she'd even had to use a bandage, and right now, "apply pressure" was about the only thing she remembered from her first aid training. Shoving the pillow against the wound, she pressed the fingertips of her free hand against his throat, searching for a pulse.

Cold, hard stone met her touch.

She frowned and ran her hand up to his ear and over the detailed strands of his hair. Everything felt as hard as stone, just like always. How the hell was he bleeding? Curious, she pulled up the pillow to look at the hole in his chest. Blood welled out of it like a geyser and a bullet emerged, plunking to the floor.

She sucked in a breath and reached for the bit of metal, holding it between two fingers. Shock and awe had taken away any scrap of revulsion that might've remained inside her. This was the slug from her rifle, all right. But it had entered the statue as if puncturing flesh, not shattering stone. She returned her gaze to the hole in his side—or what *had* been a hole. Although painted crimson with blood, the stone was as smooth as if the injury had never happened.

The bullet fell from her shaking fingers and she let out a slow breath. Squeezing her eyes shut, she muttered, "You can wake up now, Angie."

But when she opened them again, nothing had changed. It seemed she was trapped here. Trapped in a nightmare. "This isn't real. You don't have to be afraid."

She squared her shoulders and looked around the shattered remains of her parlor. Since her father's illness and death had forced her to sell off most of the valuables, she'd been buying back pieces as she could afford them. She'd had nightmares before about losing or breaking things, but never quite this vivid or extensive. Not only were the sofa's legs broken under the gargoyle's weight, her curio cabinet was open and several Hummel figurines lay smashed on the hardwood floor. The box with her grandmother's China in it had toppled and spilled.

Over the acrid smell of gunpowder and blood, the heady scent of night phlox drifted in through the open door. Did dreams include smell? She couldn't recall. Rising, she moved toward the door and flicked on the porch light, gazing into the darkness of her garden. The night air was cold across her skin, reminding her autumn was just around the corner. Outside, everything was as she remembered, right down to the freshly turned soil where she'd tucked in some strawberry runners earlier today. Except her gargoyle was definitely missing.

Looking over her shoulder, she examined the sprawling gargoyle taking up most of the parlor floor. How heavy was he? Maybe she had super human strength in this dream.

With a steadying breath, she moved back to the parlor and crouched at the thing's shoulder. Placing both hands under him, she tried to tilt him upright; he was immovable. *Fuck. Now what?*

A moth fluttered in and bumped around the light fixture overhead, one more intruder in a dream that felt too real. Scowling, she stalked to the open door and slammed it closed hard enough to rattle the house. Turning, she placed her hands on her hips and stared at her beloved Queen Anne sofa, its splintered wood legs scattered and stuffing leaking from the cushions. That piece of furniture had returned to its rightful spot in her parlor less than a month ago and had cost her almost an entire paycheck. God, when was she going to wake up? She was exhausted—could you be this exhausted in a dream? And there was so much to clean up. The vintage carpet was sticky with drying blood, not to mention the gargoyle itself.

Telling herself it was just a dream didn't lessen her heartache as she swept up broken China and shattered Hummel figurines. Such silly little things, with their cherubic faces and innocent poses, but they reminded her of happier days. One of the pieces looked like it might be fixable with a bit of glue, so she set it aside and took the rest to the bin in the kitchen.

With tears in her eyes, she returned to the parlor. She couldn't get at the carpet until she figured out how to move the gargoyle, but she could at least clean the blood off the statue. Fetching a bucket and sponge, she began scrubbing his muscular abdomen clean.

Then she saw it. His cock. His enormously rigid cock. It hadn't been that way before. Now it stood like a thick and throbbing flagpole. Back in boarding school, she'd fooled around with a guy who had a cock like this, but she'd still been a virgin and they hadn't gone all the way. To this day, she regretted not finding out what that would've been like. Maybe this was her chance? It was a dream after all. Maybe she could turn this nightmare around.

She glanced at the gargoyle's face.

He stared back at her with glowing emerald eyes.

Sten had used his stone-form to heal himself in the past, but never had he come as close to death as tonight. The bullet had caught him unaware, sending him crashing backwards as it entered his lung and lodged close against his spine. The vast amount of energy required to enter the *duramna* and staunch the bleeding took all his concentration. After so many decades standing immobile in the garden, his energy stores were already depleted. He roused from the hibernation-like state with every cell in his body crying out for sustenance.

Yet the human woman beside him was making him think of anything but food.

Her dark, nearly black hair was usually up in a messy bun while she worked in the garden, but tonight it hung in silky strands that brushed her bare shoulders. Shoulders that were very pink, very human, feminine, and soft, not angular and blocky like a Khargal female's. There was no reason he should want to run his mouth along the curve to her throat. To touch every exposed inch of her with his tongue. Except that he did. Her scent filled his nostrils, and despite his weakened condition, mating heat rose inside him. *Hondassa.*

She met his gaze and gasped, dropping her sponge and falling backward onto her bottom. Sten sat up, reaching for her, unable to take his eyes off her. Wanting to lay his hands on her. Needing to claim her in a way that should be unnatural for a Khargal. She was Earthian, for *Lar's* sake. Even without the Prime Directive ruling his interactions, he should feel no such thing for one of this planet's soft, rounded females, no matter that he was sworn to protect her bloodline.

Her bloodline. That must be the reason for his reaction.

She was, indeed, Graj's descendent. Sten had always wondered how his friend had been attracted to an Earthian all those centuries ago, compelled to not only break the Prime Directive, but reproduce. During the centuries of Sten's watch, Angie's hybrid forefathers had only produced males, and Angie's birth had made him believe she'd been sired by someone other than the aging man who claimed to be her father. When William finally died, Sten had considered his long watch ended, certain the female was purely Earthian. He'd only remained in the garden because he had nowhere else to go.

Now, in his mobile form for the first time in decades, Angie's pheromones called to him in a way he couldn't deny. His duty was far from complete. This female had to be a hybrid.

She edged away from him like a crab, muttering, "Wake up, wake up."

"I am fully awake," he assured her, clenching his fists in an attempt to quell his growing lust. Her panties and tank top left nothing to the imagination, and he needed something to satiate him before he did something rash and violated the Prime Directive even more. "I require food."

"Food?" She scrambled to her feet. "Sure. Right. I'll get you food. Be right back."

Within a few seconds, she returned with a bowl and two boxes tucked under one arm. She set the bowl on the floor a few feet away and held up the boxes. "Do gargoyles prefer Caramel-Ohs or Cinnaflakes?"

"I need meat." His kind were hunters back on Duras.

Her face turned three shades paler. "I don't have any. I usually eat at the diner."

He realized his canines were showing and forced his lips closed. "I apologize for frightening you." Standing, he folded his wings tightly to either side of his spine. "Take me to this diner."

She laughed. "Fuck, can this dream get any weirder?"

A dream. The few times he'd revealed himself to one of her ancestors, they'd had similar reactions. If he returned to his position in the garden, she might assume she'd imagined the whole thing. "I will resume my position in the garden as soon as I have eaten."

Her gaze slid toward his crotch. "I don't want to go to the diner. This is my dream and I want to do something... fun."

A waft of her pheromones reached him again, drawing his cock upright like a lure. Her breasts strained against her thin tank top, nipples jutting against the fabric. "You don't know what you ask."

"Sure I do." She moved forward, and before he knew what was happening, had wrapped her delicate hand around the base of his shaft. "I'm not a virgin anymore."

He growled low in his throat, all thoughts of food or Prime Directive evaporating. He would satiate himself in more ways than one before returning to his watch. "Are you certain?"

She licked her bottom lip and nodded, hand sliding up the length of his shaft in a way that made his entire body shudder.

In one swift move he wrapped both arms around her smaller frame and crushed her against his chest. She let out a gust of air, her pupils wide as she looked up into his face. His lips met hers in a kiss. He knew he had to be bruising her, but her moan was one of pleasure and her arms snaked up around his neck to tangle her fingers in his hair. A part of him felt guilty, like he was taking advantage of her, but the desire raging inside him refused to be denied.

She opened her mouth against his, inviting his tongue to plunge inside. She felt so warm, so alive, and her scent was like a drug. He spread his hands over her backside, careful to keep his claws retracted, and rubbed his erection against her as he ravaged her mouth. Her breasts teased his chest with their pointed tips. She threw her head back, and he brushed his lips along her jawline to her ear, licking the outer shell before burying his nose in her hair. He inhaled deeply. *Hondassa.*

The mating urge was strong. His glands swelled with the need to inject her with his *dassa*, the fluid that would bind them together. *Lar*, he wasn't here to claim a mate. But he could claim the moment, partake in a pleasure he'd never imagined finding on this planet. He pulled back, ripping her tank top down the front.

Her breasts were perfection—larger and rounder than the females of his kind. He dipped his head and latched onto one, the dark nipple puckering. As he sucked it to further hardness, she rocked her hips against him, her breath coming in tiny gasps. "I don't even know your name."

He nipped the erect nipple and moved to her other breast. "Sten."

"Sten," she moaned.

His balls tightened and his shaft grew painfully hard. He wanted inside her. He wanted to fill her, to feel her essence around him. To make her scream his name.

Securing both hands under her bottom, he lifted her, propelling her forward and pinning her against the wall. She wrapped both legs around his waist, the heat of her center directly over his cock. Her thin panties were damp against him, and the head of his shaft throbbed with a life of its own.

She slid one hand between them, pulling the crotch of her panties aside. "I want you now."

Her scent washed up between them. To plunge inside her would be heaven. But if he wanted to return to the garden and leave her satiated with the memory of a dream, he needed to be sure not to hurt her. Then she could wake from her "dream" without a physical trace.

He gritted his teeth and slowly rubbed the ribbed underside of his shaft along her slickness, bumping up over the little bud at the apex. She cried out. *Ah, her sensitive spot.* He circled the bud, using the head of his cock to tease her. Over and over again, increasing his speed, he stimulated her until she was writhing and gasping, wetness coating them both.

"Fuck me!" she cried, bucking against him.

He gave in.

The sweet embrace of her heat consumed him. Overwhelmed him. He was surprised her small frame was capable of taking all of him, but pleased, and ground his hips against her before pulling back and sliding inside again. The friction was pure ecstasy, building pressure inside him in more places than just his balls. His mating gland was threatening to burst, demanding he claim this female. He wasn't sure how much longer he could last without releasing the venom that would make her his forever. And that would most definitely not be something she could imagine dreaming.

He needed her to come. Needed her to find her pleasure so he could find his. He pounded into her, angling his hips so he banged against her clit. Her heels dug into his backside as she clung to his shoulders, mouth open in what looked like a silent scream. Then her core tightened and her eyes flew open, meeting his gaze. The pulsing rhythm of her climax drove him over the edge.

With a roar, he let loose his orgasm, driving into her even deeper, every muscle in his body shuddering with release. The force of his ejaculation seemed to catapult her into a new frenzy, and her fingertips dug into his skin as she screamed his name. With a shuddering exhale, she slumped against him. For a moment, he feared maybe he'd killed her. Then she sighed and wrapped both arms loosely around his neck, murmuring into his neck, "Best. Nightmare. Ever."

Angie leaned her cheek against her statue's hard chest, barely able to catch her breath. He smelled divine, both salty and sweet in a way that felt addictive. She hoped she didn't wake up anytime soon; as soon as she had her strength back, she wanted to be with him again.

Sten shifted away from the wall, holding her against his chest. One huge hand cradled the back of her head as he murmured words she couldn't understand into her hair. He carried her through the door toward the stairs, but when he reached the bottom step, he swayed and his grip slackened.

She released her legs from around his waist. "Are you okay?"

The light from the parlor glowed through his leathery wings as they stretched into an impressive span behind his back. His upper lip curled, revealing the sharp teeth she'd spotted earlier. "I must hunt."

A spike of fear lanced through her. "Hunt? For what?"

He swayed again, bracing himself with one hand on the banister. "At this point, anything I can catch."

Angie swallowed. That was what she was afraid of. "If you need protein, I have a can of tuna in the cupboards." She shifted to edge past him. "Let me get it."

He blocked her, one hand cupping her face and stroking a clawed thumb over her cheek. "Go to your bed, *Hondassa*. When you wake, all will be as it was."

For some reason, the claw gave her a shiver that wasn't entirely fear. What was that word he kept saying? "What does *Hondassa* mean?"

A pained expression pinched his features, and he dropped his hand. "Nothing of importance."

She looked past him into the parlor. To her left, the rifle lay at the base of the stairs exactly where she'd set it. Things were too exact. Too consistent. Was she really dreaming? Pulse beating hard in her throat, she pinched the skin on her forearm hard enough to make herself flinch. "I'm not asleep." She frowned up into his face. "This isn't a dream, is it?"

"It is as you believe it to be." His eyes tightened, as if he was desperate for her to agree.

Lifting both hands, she placed them flat against his chest, ran them down his abs, stopping short at his waist. Below her palms, his cock rose as if anticipating her touch. Her heartbeat sped up. She'd just had sex with a gargoyle. A living, breathing gargoyle. "This is real." She met his eyes once more, pulling sharply away. "You're alive. How?"

He edged backward toward the door. "You would not believe me if I told you."

She was trembling, every instinct in her body telling her to flee. And yet, there was no way in hell she was going to let him leave without answering some questions. Without taking her eyes off him, she bent to retrieve her rifle and aimed it at him. "Stop. You're not going anywhere until you tell me who you are and what's going on."

Raising both hands, he said, "There is no need to fear me. I have safeguarded your family for generations."

"You broke into my house!"

He tilted his head. "You shot me."

She raised her brows. "Because you broke into my house."

"Acknowledged. Although to be fair, I only entered in pursuit of another man."

She glanced toward the closed exterior door. She'd almost forgotten there'd been a second person here when she came down the stairs. "My dad used to tell me the family had a guardian angel." She surveyed the clawed wings rising above his shoulders. "You don't look like an angel."

"I am not an angel." He retracted his wings until she could no longer see them. "But I am here to watch over you."

"Really?" She narrowed her eyes. "You told me I was dreaming, then proceeded to take advantage of me. How's that watching over me?"

His gray-skinned face darkened. "You are the one who said you were dreaming. I simply did not deny it. And I did not initiate the interaction."

"But you went along and let me think it was a dream."

Lowering his head, he nodded. "You are correct. Loss of blood must have weakened my restraint. I apologize."

"You can apologize by telling me who you are and what you're doing here."

His teeth flashed with predatory sharpness. "If I do not have sustenance soon, I will not be able to tell you anything."

He sagged to one knee, one hand pressed over the spot where his wound had been.

Realizing he was grimacing, not trying to threaten her, she lowered her rifle. "I should call an ambulance for you, but I don't know what they'll do."

That seemed to rouse him, and this time his bared teeth were aggressive. "Do not call your authorities. You will undo everything I have worked for."

Stomach once more clenching in alarm, she asked, "Worked for? What do you mean?"

"There are entities on this planet that would kill to get their hands on me. And on you. Do not call the authorities. I will heal with time."

Regardless of how scary Sten looked, she didn't think he meant her any harm. And her father had always spoken as if the family guardian was real. She wondered if he'd ever had an encounter like this, though. Well, not exactly like this. Remembering their passion, she sighed. She didn't have anything resembling meat in the house except for tuna. "Stay here. I'll get the tuna."

Sten leaned forward, bracing himself with his free hand on the floorboards, and nodded.

Turning, she rushed to her kitchen. She hadn't had much money for groceries recently, especially after buying the sofa. *The now broken sofa,* she reminded herself, but then shook off her anger. Sten claimed he'd been after an intruder. For all she knew, he'd prevented her from being murdered in her bed. The sofa was a small price to pay.

She flung open the door to the kitchen pantry. The shelves held a few jars of garden vegetables, a tin of coffee, a bag of dried pinto beans, and two cans of tuna. She hated fish and had bought the tuna as a treat for the cat. But Sten wanted meat, and tuna was all she had.

Opening both cans, she upended them into a bowl, juice and all, wrinkling her nose at the smell. Did he like mayo or relish? She pictured him hunting down a deer and tearing into it raw with those fierce teeth of his. He might not like the fact the fish was cooked, let alone condiments. She decided not to doctor it unless he asked. Before heading back, she grabbed her apron and put it on to cover her torn tank top. She felt like a French maid in a porno, but at least her tits were no longer hanging out.

Back in the parlor, Sten sagged on the floor near the exit, his wings curled around him. Next to him, both boxes of cereal lay on their sides, a few crushed flakes scattered over the hardwood floor.

He turned his head to meet her gaze. "These Caramel-Ohs lack nutritional value."

Suppressing a laugh, she set the tuna on the floor next to him. "You sound like the Menu Planner at my boarding school. Here. It's tuna. I have mayo and relish if you'd—"

He snatched up the bowl and upended it into his mouth, downing the contents in what appeared to be a single gulp. Then he cocked his head at the bowl and took a huge bite out of the ceramic.

"Hey! That's my Fiesta Ware!"

His teeth crunched loudly, and he swallowed. "It contains minerals to assist my healing."

She watched in horror as he took another bite from the bowl. Then he reached for the broken Hummel figurine she'd set next to the curio cabinet. She lunged forward. "No! Stop!"

He cocked his head. "Do you have other materials I may consume?"

She thought of the broken figurines she'd dumped in the waste bin and sighed. They were garbage anyway. At least if he ate them, they'd go to good use. "Don't touch anything. I'll be right back."

Rushing to the kitchen, she pulled out the bin. She'd changed the bag before bed last night, and the only things in it were the broken figurines. Retrieving the largest pieces, she set them on the counter one by one, part of her returning to thinking she must be in a dream. Either that, or the kickback from the rifle had given her a concussion. She felt someone watching her and looked up to find Sten leaning against the doorframe. The look in his eyes was definitely hungry, but she got the sensation it might be for something other than food. Or pottery.

She gestured toward the pieces on the counter. "You can eat these."

He moved forward, his gaze never leaving hers. His presence seemed to fill the room, forcing her back a step until she bumped into the sink. Slowly, he picked up a shard, crunching robotically.

"Does it taste… good?" She couldn't believe any of this was happening. But she couldn't deny how real the naked, hot-as-hell, pottery-eating gargoyle in front of her was, either.

His voice was more gravelly than usual when he replied, "The minerals are sufficient for now. However, the sodium content in your meat has made me thirsty."

She turned to the cupboard and selected a tall glass, filling it with tap water before handing it to him. "Please don't eat my glass."

He eyed the water. "Much like your Caramel-Ohs, there is little nutritional value in glass."

"Oh." She watched his muscular throat move as he swallowed the water. Tiny spur-like protrusions on his jawline reminded her once more she wasn't looking at a man, but damn, he was sexy.

He set the empty glass carefully on the countertop, his emerald eyes seeming to cloud over. "The *duramna* is trying to claim me once more."

"What's that?"

"My healing form, much like the one I held in your garden."

She put a hand on his forearm, suddenly worried he'd go back to being a statue without answering her questions. "Don't go yet."

"Unless you have more food for me, I must rest."

"I have vegetables or dried beans." She moved to the pantry and held up the bag. "Beans have protein like meat, but they take time to soak and cook."

"I have had beans before. They are quite nutritious." He snatched the bag from her. Hooking through one corner of the plastic with a clawed forefinger, he tore it open and poured several beans into his mouth.

Was there anything this guy actually considered inedible? After a few moments of him crunching loudly with his eyes closed, she ventured, "They're much better cooked."

He opened his eyes. "Thank you for your concern. I will return to the garden now."

"Not so fast! You owe me an explanation."

He ran his claws through his hair and stared up at the ceiling. "I cannot break our Prime Directive."

"Prime Directive? Like in Star Trek?" She looked pointedly at his crotch. "I think you've already broken that tonight."

His color darkened. "You are correct."

"Why don't you start by telling me what you are."

"Humans call us gargoyles."

It felt like there had to be another shoe about to drop, but he didn't volunteer anything else. She put her hands on her hips. "Clever. But what are you really?"

He let out a sigh. "I am a Khargal. When my ship crashed on your planet, our *duramna* allowed us to hide amidst the stone statues your kind creates."

"But my father said his grandfather brought our statue— you—over on a frigate back in the days before steam engines. You can't be that old."

"I have been here a long time. Your legends of gargoyles came to be because of us." Sten pressed his lips together and took a deep breath. "Some of my kind attempted to assimilate and even found mates, including my friend, Graj. I swore an oath to protect his lineage."

It took her a moment to process what he was saying. "His... lineage?" Sten was in her garden. He protected her family. "As in descendants? Are my family descendants of a... a Khargal?" Aliens and living statues were hard enough to swallow. But this?

He pointed toward her throat. "Do you know what that is?"

She looked down, then realized he was referring to her pendant. "My dad gave it to my mom as a wedding gift."

"But he never explained its origins?"

She shook her head.

Sten hooked the silver chain tenderly with one claw, lifting the pendant off her skin. "It is one of our sigils. A communication device carried by every one of the Khargals on board the ship when it crashed. I have one just like it hidden in your garden."

Her fingers touched the pendant gently. "I feel like I must be dreaming again."

"You are not." He sank into a crouch, resting forward on one hand.

She frowned. "Would you like to rest on the sofa…" then she remembered she didn't have a sofa any more.

"I must return to your garden and resume my *duramna*. No one must know I am other than I seem."

"You mean go back to being a statue? But I have more questions." She put a hand on his muscular shoulder as if she could physically keep him in place.

"Join me in the garden." He placed a huge clawed hand over hers, his emerald eyes intense. "I will tell you all I can before the *duramna* takes me."

Sten stepped into the pleasantly cool night air, his need to rest and heal becoming more difficult to ignore, even with Angie's alluring, half-naked body so close to him. He trailed the backs of his claws over the tops of the nearby foliage as he followed Angie off the porch. "I am in awe of your ability to nurture these plants. You would do well on Duras. The climate there is much like it is in these mountains."

"Duras is the name of your planet?" She stopped at the stone bench next to where he'd stood watch for almost three generations. "Do you want to sit here to talk?"

The Prime Directive made his throat tighten as he regarded her casual invitation. Sitting next to an Earthian and discussing his people was forbidden. It went against every bit of training he'd undergone. But he'd been marooned on this planet over a thousand years with no hope of rescue. Why should he remain bereft of companionship or comfort when *Lar* had sent him a *Hondassa*?

She was sweeter than anything he could have imagined and he would tell her anything she wanted to know. Give her anything she desired. He'd kept the Prime Directive long enough. He moved toward the bench. "As you wish."

He settled onto the center of the seat, tucking his tail in behind one leg. Angie seemed uncertain as she looked at the remaining space on either side of him. She was a mouth-watering sight in that silly apron over her almost non-existent night clothes, clutching her elbows over her chest. In the darkness, his enhanced vision detected tiny bumps along her skin. The late September weather did not affect him, but Earthians would consider it chilly. "Are you cold?"

She shrugged. "Not exactly."

Gesturing to the bench, he spread his wings. "I shall shelter you."

She shook her head, but took a seat next to him. "Sexy and poetic. Are you certain I'm not dreaming?"

With a chuckle, he pulled her closer, cocooning her with his wing. She was so small, so frail, his urge to protect her from harm surged beyond mere duty. There was nothing else that mattered half as much.

"That man who was in the garden," he said. "Did he say who he represented?" He'd only been partially awake for the conversation, brought alert by the man's touch.

Angie shrugged. "I didn't ask. He gave me a card, but I didn't keep it. Was he the one who broke in?"

"No, it was a different Earthian. But it is a strange coincidence."

"Earthian. That's what you you call humans?"

He nodded once. "Yes. Human."

"Cute. So, I thought that guy wanted my gargoyle—you. Why break in?"

Sten reached over and touched the pendant nestled at her throat. "He may have seen your pendant and recognized it. There is a society of humans who have pursued my kind—*our* kind—for centuries, seeking knowledge of our technology. Men like them are the very reason we have a Prime Directive. Was there a symbol on the card? A flower of some type?"

"I didn't look."

He sighed. "You must be cautious. If these men I speak of discover you have Khargal blood, they will not be so easily chased away."

"I'm still not buying this whole part-alien thing." She rubbed her fingertips along her forehead. "I don't have even a hint of horns, let alone wings or a tail. Neither did my dad."

"On the contrary, your father had a residual tail which the doctor removed at birth. Your family's Khargal attributes have subsided with the introduction of more human blood over the generations. After so many births of exclusively males, I believed a female might be impossible. Then you were born, and I assumed the bloodline had ended."

"But if I have kids…" She stiffened against his side, her brows pinching. "Wait, are you saying you thought I wasn't my father's biological child?"

"The possibility crossed my mind. However, I know that is not the case, now. You have Khargal blood."

"How do you know?"

He turned his head to look into her eyes. "There is no other explanation for the feelings I have."

"What kind of… feelings?" Her scent changed, arousal spiking the air.

Macero, she was ready for him at barely a word. He could no longer deny that Angie was his *Hondassa*, regardless of how much Earthian DNA she had. His cock stirred, urging him to mate again, to claim her despite the need to shift to his *duramna*. "Khargals are sensitive to pheromonal connections, a way of discerning which partner has the potential to be a true mate. Finding a match is rare, even between Khargals."

He let his words sink in, conscious of her wide-eyed stare beneath his wing.

The silence grew heavy. His eyes ached and skin itched with the need to shift. Finally, Angie spoke. "You're saying you think I'm your… true mate."

"Do not worry. I would never give you the venom without your permission."

"Venom?" She shot to her feet, pulling free of his wing with a sharp twist. "What's this about venom? Are you a vampire? An alien gargoyle is weird enough for one night."

"Nothing like a vampire. I chose the wrong Earthian word. In Durassian we call it *dassa*." He pulled his wings against his back, trying to appear as non-threatening as possible. "Mates share the *dassa* bond at a cellular level. It allows them to procreate, grants a longer life, and other benefits."

The stiffness in her shoulders relaxed. "So to have a baby, my ancestors shared this *dassa*?"

"Yes. If your female ancestor had not been killed by her own kind, she would have lived alongside Graj for many centuries."

Angie licked her lips in a way that made his cock stir again. "So Graj was… my great-whatever grandfather? How did that happen?"

"Yes, Graj is the Khargal who sired your family bloodline." Taking a deep breath, he called to mind those days, centuries ago, when he and his crew mates had gone their separate ways, trying to hide from the Earthians hunting them. "When my ship first arrived on your planet, your kind believed we were demons. Those of us who were not killed were forced into hiding. Graj was a science officer and specialized in primitive alien cultures; Earthian cities were a lure to him. He had a perception filter that could disguise him as an Earthian—a human—and often scouted alleys and brothels during the black of night. There was one particular woman he liked to watch. Then one night, he revealed himself to her. He believed he'd found his *Hondassa*."

"There's that word you keep using."

Sten looked at the sky. The horizon had developed a lavender cast with the coming dawn, reminding him of the violet skies of home. "It means true mate."

"Oh." She settled to the bench at his side once more.

A thrill ran through Sten at her choosing to be close once more, and he wrapped her in his wing. "Is this all right?"

"Yes. Please, tell me more."

"As you wish." A tingling warmth spread from her skin to his. "Graj and his *Hondassa* enjoyed many years together. He had been elated to discover his *Hondassa* was a compatible species to produce offspring." The memory of his friend's joy was still etched in Sten's memory. "But while he could use his perception filter to hide among your people, he did not have a second device for the youngling. The child had a Khargal's tail. The midwife wanted to smother it immediately. Instead, Graj and his mate kept the youngling swaddled to hide the difference. Within a few months, the babe's horn buds and wings emerged, however. Those were more difficult to hide.

"I suggested Graj move his family far away. Find a place where no Earthians dwelled. But his *Hondassa* had ailing parents and did not want to leave. And she would not allow Graj to take away her baby." Sten squeezed his eyes shut. He had not brought Graj to mind in many years, and the story was just as painful as he remembered.

"So what did they do?"

He pulled his wing closer, needing to feel Angie's warmth. "For a time, Graj and his mate kept the child indoors, away from human eyes. But one day a priest came to attend the ailing grandparents and spied the child. He accused the woman of consorting with demons. A mob gathered and captured Graj's mate and child, intending to burn them at the stake."

"Oh my God!" Angie threaded her fingers through his.

Sten kept going, needing to release a story he'd not told to anyone until now. "Graj and I attempted to breach the prison and retrieve both mate and child. I succeeded with the child. Graj… did not."

Never had he carried a burden so heavy as he had that day he left the city with a crying child in his arms, the sound of screaming Earthians, roaring flames, and shattering Khargal stone fading into the distance. The memory made Sten feel as brittle as shale, and the *duramna* was forcing him into darkness. He could no longer hold back the instinct to rest.

"I am unable to speak on this more." He withdrew his wing and rose, turning to offer her a hand. "But I will come to you after dark to speak again if you'd like."

She accepted his grip, standing to face him. "I would."

Dawn peeked over the horizon, painting her soft skin in pastel light and catching the facets of the ruby-colored pendant at her throat. He touched a claw to it. "The Rose Syndicate may approach you again. Do not allow this sigil out of your possession."

Her hand rose, hiding the pendant from his sight. "It was my mother's. I never take it off. Even if you hadn't told me what it is, I'd never let that asshat touch it."

He smiled, amused by how protective she was to the things she considered hers. He bent, brushing his mouth over hers in the gesture of affection Earthians called a kiss. She leaned into him, her breath sweet as the nectar of the flowers surrounding them, her lips as soft as petals. His fangs ached, urging him to finalize the claim on his *Hondassa*. But she was not ready for that—if she ever would be—and he needed to sleep and heal. "I will be very hungry again when I wake."

"I'll bring back something from the diner."

He gave her a sideways smile. "Perhaps I will need more than food."

The flush infusing her pink skin gratified him. He turned and stepped over the mounds of flowers, adjusting himself to hide his erection before turning to stone.

🙚🙚🙘

Winston York the Third was an analyst, not a field agent, and he'd never seen an alien personally, but the statue in that woman's yard matched every description he'd ever read of the creatures. Then he'd seen the woman's necklace, that egg-shaped ruby gem every member of the Rose Syndicate was instructed to look for, and he knew the statue was no mere coincidental likeness.

He'd found a real gargoyle.

Out here, in the middle of nowhere Montana.

Who would've thought such a thing was even possible?

He stood in one corner of his room at the bed-and-breakfast, trying not to move and lose the connection. Cell service out here was atrocious. "The burglar you connected me to was a buffoon." The man had left a message on York's voicemail about monsters and armed guards. When York tried to call him back, he got no answer. "All he succeeded in doing was alerting the target."

"We'll take care of him. Meanwhile, keep your head low until we can get a full team out there."

"When do you think that will be? Hello?" He wasn't sure if she'd hung up or if the connection had been disrupted. Either way, he wasn't going to just sit on his hands. He'd seen a pair of binoculars in the pawn shop. He was going to keep an eye on that statue.

A ngie watched Sten resume his half-crouch over her marigolds. In the pale dawn light, it looked as if he'd never moved. The casual observer might not notice the tilt of his shoulders had changed, or that the slight pattern of curls in his hair was different. She wondered how many times he'd moved over the years and she'd never noticed.

Edging closer, she stopped directly in front of Sten's face, looking into his vacant stone eyes. With tentative fingers, she traced the side of his cheek and one perfectly sculpted biceps. His limbs were hard and cold, yet somehow not dead feeling. He was living stone, and an instinctive part of her could sense the life surging beneath his rocky exterior.

From inside the house, the gong from her grandfather clock reminded her it was time to get ready for her shift. Forcing herself to turn away, she trudged back inside to shower and dress in something besides her panties and an apron. Good thing she didn't have neighbors to notice her attire on their way to work.

While she dressed, she stood at the window over-looking the garden. She'd been confronted with so many things in a short amount of time, she felt like she was going crazy. Only she wasn't. The encounter with Sten had been too real. Things could never go back to the way they were now that she knew about him. *And had sex with him.* Yeah, don't forget that part. Her pussy tingled when she thought about the way he'd filled her.

The doorbell interrupted her thoughts. She must be running even further behind than she thought; Mae usually honked to let her know she was waiting in her truck. Unless she'd brought extra eggs over and was letting herself inside…

The parlor! Angie flew down the stairs two at a time, grabbing the end of the banister with one hand to keep from slamming into the wall.

Too late. Mae had used her key and was already inside, egg carton about to fall out of her hand as she gaped at the mess. "What happened here?"

Angie cringed. The parlor looked even worse in daylight. The collapsed sofa was bad enough, but the huge, red stain on the area rug looked like the scene of a murder. How was she going to explain that away? "Someone broke into my house last night."

"That's a lot of blood." Mae couldn't seem to take her eyes off the stain on the floor.

Angie tried to think of an excuse, but all she could come up with was, "It's not mine."

Mae's eyes widened. "Did you kill someone? Where is he?"

"He ran away." At least she could tell the truth about that. "I think it may've been some creepy dude who came by yesterday wanting to buy my gargoyle."

"Did you call the police?"

"Not yet. Thanks for the eggs." Angie swept the carton out of Mae's grip, torn between wanting to get Mae out of here and needing to act normal. She headed through the dining room to the kitchen to shove the eggs into the fridge.

"What? Why not?" Mae followed close behind, running a hand through her short hair as she scanned all the corners as if expecting an attack. "Did anything get stolen?

"I'm not sure yet," Angie answered truthfully, holding open the kitchen's side door. The less time spent inside, the better. "But a lot of stuff got broken. Come on. If I'm late, Robert will give me hell."

Hurrying toward the wrought-iron gate, Angie had a hard time ignoring Sten as she passed him by. Was he watching her? She climbed into the passenger side of Mae's pickup and pulled the door closed.

Mae slid in behind the wheel. "Wow, I can't believe you had someone break in. Sheriff Rollands is going to be thrilled to have a case." Mae shot her a sideways glance and Angie snorted. Everyone knew the sheriff hated anything that created paperwork. Mae started the engine. "I'll come help you clean tonight."

"That's okay. It's only the parlor. I can manage." The last thing Angie wanted was Mae showing up while Sten was awake.

"That's what friends are for." She pulled away from the curb. "I'll bring tequila."

"No, really. You don't need to come over." Angie floundered for a believable excuse. "I have to harvest the seeds from my heirloom peas before the crows get them and I have tomato seeds fermenting that I need to sort and dry before they sprout."

"Really? You're going to leave that blood stain on your floor just to gather seeds? You know you can just buy those, right?" Mae down-shifted at the steepest part of the switch-back and rounded the corner. "Bloodstains are hard to get out. I should know." Mae was a nurse at the town's only clinic and was always complaining about the bodily fluids she had to clean out of her clothes.

Angie put a hand against the dash to brace herself for the turn. "It's not the same. My great grandma brought that variety with her from Pennsylvania."

Mae shook her head. "You are a seriously crazy woman."

Relieved at leaving the topic of the break-in behind, Angie laughed. "You know me well. Hey, did you eat yet? Let me out at the door and I'll grab you a couple of pieces of bacon for the road."

"If you're offering bacon, it doesn't matter if I ate yet or not."

"And you call yourself a doctor."

"Nurse Practitioner, thank you very much."

Ahead, the road entered the streets of New Turnbull. The buildings were designed to look like the old west, lining Main Street with two-story facades and fancy wooden boardwalks instead of concrete. The diner's plate-glass windows had gold scrollwork painted in the corners and an old-timey menu posted out front to attract tourists. Although it was barely seven a.m., the slanted parking out front held more than a handful of pickup trucks.

Mae pulled into an open space, and Angie hardly waited for the wheels to stop rolling before she was out on the pavement. "Be right back."

Glancing inside the diner's front window as she neared the door, she met Robert's scowling gaze. He was pouring coffee for one of the regulars, and the cranky cook hated serving coffee. Apparently the new server was late.

She pushed past the hostess station, inhaling the peppery scent of breakfast sausage and patting one of the regulars on the shoulder as she passed. "Hey, Kyle."

"Mornin' Angie."

Robert followed her into the kitchen. "You gotta fire that new girl."

Angie raised a brow. Celia was the owner's granddaughter, and no way was Angie going to step on toes there. "Not my job."

He rolled a few sausages over on the grill. "Someone's gotta talk to her, at least."

"Well, it's not going to be me." She eyed the sausages. "Any bacon I could swipe? I gotta pay for my ride."

Robert grinned. "You'll talk to the new girl?"

Angie rolled her eyes. "I'll mention it to Mrs. Hendricks when she comes in later." Robert tossed two sausages onto a plate. Angie made a face. "Bacon?"

"Beggars can't be choosers." He reached for a couple of eggs. "Hurry it up. Kyle's been here twenty minutes already."

Sighing, Angie took the sausages and hurried past the tables to Mae's truck out front. Mae frowned at the sausages. "You promised bacon."

Angie picked up a link and took a bite. "If you don't want them…"

"Fine." Mae reached out the window and snagged the other sausage. "I'll pick you up after your shift." Shifting into reverse, she headed down the street toward the clinic.

Back inside, Angie went through the first half of her shift on autopilot, thoughts consumed by imagining what Sten was doing back at the house. Her hand kept reaching for the pendant at her throat. Her father'd told her plenty of stories about his childhood and the family's past, but the only mention of the gargoyle had been how it'd come with them from Europe two hundred years ago. Sten was their oldest family heirloom. And he was a living being. Could he really be that old?

Sometime around noon, Mrs. Hendricks came in, heading to her usual table near the window without waiting to be seated. As always, she was dressed far too well for their podunk town, hanging her Louis Vuitton handbag over the corner of her chair before she sat. Her hair had been freshly colored that brassy shade of red many women her age seemed to favor. Angie grabbed the coffee pot and headed over to fill her cup. "What can I get you for lunch today?"

"Turkey club, extra mayo." Mrs. Hendricks used her manicured red nails to carefully open three creamers and poured them into her cup.

"Coming right up." Angie turned to go but was halted by a hand on her arm.

Mrs. Hendricks had her smug Historical Society smile in place. "I have a wealthy benefactor asking for a personal tour of Old Turnbull. Would you mind if we dropped in for a look through your house later this afternoon?"

"That's not a good idea." Angie scrambled to think of a

reason to say no. "I have a lot of clean up to do. I had a break in last night." As soon as she said it, she regretted it.

"Oh, dear, you had a break-in?" Mrs. Hendricks crepe-papery eyes widened. "I just saw Sheriff Rollands, and he didn't mention it."

Angie faked a wide smile and waved a nonchalant hand in the air. "It was nothing. Just a few of my knick-knacks were broken." She hated calling her heirlooms knick-knacks, but she didn't want Mrs. Hendricks to be alarmed over anything she might consider of historical value. "I just need time to clean up."

"Was the house damaged?" Mrs Hendricks pursed her lips. As the head of the Historical Society, she'd already cited Angie for taking too long to repair a broken window. Not that the rest of the ghost town didn't look like shit, but whatever.

"The house is fine. And the vandals ran off." Angie felt fairly proud of herself for thinking of that detail on the spur of the moment. "No need to file a report."

Mrs. Hendricks let out an exasperated breath and reached around her chair for her purse. "I'm calling the sheriff. If there is one thing we won't stand for here in Turnbull, it's crime. You go on home, dear. I'll have him meet you there."

Much as Angie would like to go home, the last thing she needed was a visit from the sheriff. "I can't leave, Mrs. Hendricks. Celia didn't show up for her shift today."

Mrs. Hendricks stiffened, blinking twice before frowning. "Well, I'll just see to that nonsense right now."

Angie backed away as the woman dialed her granddaughter. Robert would be pleased, and hopefully Mrs. Hendricks would forget all about calling the sheriff.

No such luck. When Angie brought the sandwich to the table, Mrs. Hendricks said, "Celia will be here any minute, dear. And I've let the sheriff know about the break-in. You get your things and go meet him at your house."

Balling her fists at her sides, Angie nodded and retreated to the kitchen. At the grill, Robert's usual scowl softened. "You okay?"

"I told Mrs. Hendricks about Celia." Angie gave him a tight-lipped smile. "The girl is on her way in to take over. I have to go meet the sheriff at my place."

"You in some sort of trouble?"

Robert came across as gruff, but he wasn't a bad guy. She shook her head. "It's nothing. I'll be in tomorrow."

She hung her apron, grabbed her purse, and rushed outside before remembering she'd promised to bring food back for Sten. *Shit*. As she turned to go back inside to beg a plate of food, she nearly ran into Mr. York. He gave her an oily smile. "Just the person I was hoping to see."

Straightening her shoulders, she shook her head. His stupid attempt to buy her house was the last thing she had time to think about. "Sorry, I have to go."

She spun on her heel and strode down the boardwalk. Now not only would she have to walk home, she'd be forced to get food from the gas station mini-mart on the way. She bought two cans of baked beans, a package of hot dogs, and a loaf of bread. Not exactly the kind of home-cooked meal she'd imagined for Sten, but he'd liked dried beans last night, so this could only be an improvement.

Sweat was running down her sides by the time she reached the top of the first switchback on the hill, and she was feeling her lack of sleep in every muscle. She huffed past the old schoolhouse that now served as a pitiful excuse for a mining museum and rounded the corner onto what had once been Main Street in the old town. Ahead, parked just outside her wrought-iron fence, the sheriff's Bronco waited.

Shit. She'd hoped to beat him there and throw a rug or something over the blood stain. She picked up her pace, pointedly keeping her gaze off of her gargoyle as she passed through the yard. Rollands was kicked back on her porch swing, hat tilted to cover his face, hands clasped over his scrawny belly.

She moved quietly up the steps, hoping to sneak past him before he knew she was there, but he lifted the brim of his hat with one finger. "Thought you'd be here a while ago."

"I had to walk." She attempted a smile, holding up the grocery bag. "Give me a second to put this away and I'll be right out." Maybe she could throw a towel over the stain, or better yet, give him a report without letting him inside.

He rose, hooking both thumbs into his belt loops. "Already took a peek through the glass." He twitched his head toward the parlor's bay window without breaking eye contact. "Looks like you had quite a night last night."

Her stomach dropped. She hadn't even considered he might look through the windows. "The intruder ran off. No need to worry."

"Pretty good-sized blood stain in there. I'm going to need to have a look."

He'd already seen the blood stain, so what did she have to lose? Nodding, she led the way up the steps and unlocked the front door, leading him into the ransacked parlor.

Rollands stood looking over the mess with his hands on his hips. "Can you describe the guy?"

She shook her head, trying to remember the events of last night. "It was dark. I yelled out that I had a gun, and when I came downstairs, something huge lunged at me. So I fired. Then the intruder ran out of the open door."

Rollands pulled his phone from his breast pocket and took several photos of the mess. "He broke your sofa? Must've been a really big fellow."

"Yeah. And he broke a bunch of my figurines." She pointed to the half-empty curio cabinet before realizing her mistake. Sten had eaten the ceramics, so she had no proof they'd even existed, let alone been broken. She picked up the one she intended to glue back together. "See?"

"Anything taken?"

"I don't think so, or I'd've called you."

The sheriff seemed to be appeased by her answer and tucked his phone back into his breast pocket. "I haven't had any reports of someone coming in with a gunshot wound." He pulled a swab kit from his back pocket and dabbed at the stain. "I'll need to give a sample to the lab to see if it's human."

The pressure in Angie's chest eased. *The blood isn't human.* This could be the solution to everything. "Could it have been a bear? I was exhausted from gardening and might've left my front door ajar."

He scratched his head. "Coulda been. You said it was dark. And a couple of hikers reported seeing one last week." He stepped over one of the broken sofa legs and moved toward the door. "You want to file a report?"

Angie found herself shaking her head, for once glad the sheriff didn't like paperwork.

"Well, let me know if you're missing any valuables."

"Of course." She beamed at him. "Thank you."

She saw him to the foyer and onto the porch, watching him drive away in a cloud of dust. Finally, she was alone with her gargoyle.

❧ 6 ❧

Angie pulled the dry husks of her grandmother's heirloom peas off the withering vines and shook them into the jar in her heirloom seed box, then moved on to divide her peonies. Mom used to grow the fragrant pink flowers next to the kitchen window, but the contractor who'd fixed her roof had crushed most of the crowns. She'd missed the cotton candy scent this spring, but luckily one plant was enough to reestablish the bed within a few years.

She puttered around outside until the sun was below the horizon and it became too difficult to see. Sten hadn't moved at all, not one flutter of an eyelid as far as she could tell. Could he see and hear her while he was a statue? She positioned herself directly in front of his stony face. "Hey. You awake in there?"

No response.

She put a hand against his cheek, staring into each of the

46

blank gray eyes in turn. He'd said he healed while in this state. Perhaps he'd been more gravely injured than he thought and needed more time. She pressed her forehead against his. "I'm going inside to make food."

Not that opening baked beans and cutting up hot dogs before throwing everything in the microwave would take a lot of time, but she didn't want any distractions when he came inside. He had a lot more to tell her, not to mention his last words about wanting more than food. She couldn't stop thinking about the way his body had felt against hers. Inside hers. She wanted to do that again. And again.

Thinking of getting naked with him made her realize how sweaty and dusty she was, so she headed up to the shower. She'd just rinsed the lather from her hair when she heard a heavy footstep enter the room. On the other side of the stall's hazy glass, a large figure blocked the light from her bedroom doorway.

"Sten?" She turned off the water and cracked open the stall door for a peek.

Sten stood in the doorway, huge and gray, emerald eyes glittering and tail twitching. He took a halting step forward as if fighting his own body. "You are naked."

"Well, yeah. I'm in the shower." Her gaze lowered to his waistline, and she swallowed at the sight of his engorged cock. "You're naked, too."

He took another step. "The urge to mate with you is strong."

Heat flooded between her thighs and she sucked in a small breath, clinging to the edge of the stall door for support. "I thought you'd want to eat first."

"I do." He took one more stride and pulled the door from her grasp, swinging it wide. "But your arousal is impossible to ignore. I would like to taste it."

She gaped up at him as he reached in and encircled her waist with one huge arm, pulling her from the stream of water. His rock-hard body against hers made her tingle in all the right places. She found herself nodding, and he carried her back into the bedroom. He lowered her onto the bed and urged her onto her back, planting one knee between her thighs before brushing his lips against hers. "Humans call this kissing, correct?"

Her skin tingled from his touch, and the strangely salty-sweet flavor flooded her mouth. "A real kiss lasts longer. Let me show you."

She put her hand behind his neck and pulled him close, opening her mouth against his. He entwined his tongue with hers until she was left panting. For someone unfamiliar with kissing, he sure was good at it. He moved his knee against her pussy, rocking against her with an exquisite pulsing rhythm. She ground herself against him as he lavished her mouth with attention. With one hand, he cupped her breast, kneading it until her nipple couldn't possibly get any tighter. Then he broke the kiss and moved his mouth to claim her areola.

The pleasure was so intense it was almost painful, and she cried out, tangling both hands into the hair at the base of his neck. He moved to the other breast, suckling and caressing until she was on fire. She bucked her hips against his rock-hard thigh, needing more. In a move so swift it shocked her, he dropped to his knees on the floor, pulling her hips toward his face. His flat, wide tongue smoothed a languid stroke over her opening before delving into the cleft with a determination that made her back arch. She cried out, "Oh!"

His tongue made a lazy circle around her clit, easing her folds aside as he lapped against her pussy like a cat enjoying cream. Her orgasm rose with a suddenness that made her eyes fly open, and just as she was about to topple over the edge, he plunged the tip of his tail inside her. She made a strangled noise, fists clutching the bedspread to either side of her as the world seemed to tilt on its axis. Oh, good lord, his tail. And he knew how to use it. Wave after wave of searing pleasure shook her, her thighs trembling uncontrollably as he sent her skyrocketing beyond anything she'd ever experienced.

As her trembling subsided, he pressed gentle kisses against her inner thigh, hands supporting her hips. She let out a long breath, her eyes heavy as he once more rose up onto the bed to hover over her. His wings had emerged, and now gently fanned the air around them. "You are more than I ever hoped for."

She smiled languidly up at him and wrapped both ankles around his backside, urging him toward her. He adjusted himself until the head of his cock probed her opening then slowly settled into her, his heated length creating another wave of pleasure. He lay on top of her, and she nuzzled the crook of his neck. His skin felt like fine leather, smooth and hard, yet pliable and warm, and his scent filled her with urges beyond the desire for sex. As if she needed to consume every part of him. Playfully, she set her teeth against his stone-hard muscle.

He inhaled sharply, his cock seeming to swell within her. *He likes that.* Fingers digging into his back, she bit down. His wings snapped out, and he froze, a low growl rolling through him.

She eased up on the bite. "Sorry."

He pulled back, the ridges of his shaft stroking her inner walls and thrust forward again. "More."

Then someone called her name from the hallway.

"Angie?" Mae's voice grew louder. "Where are you?"

Sten pulled away from his *Hondassa* and faced the door, tail swishing with agitation. This was the most inopportune moment to interrupt, and not just because his body ached to relieve himself within Angie's warm and willing depths.

Angie had just claimed him.

It'd never occurred to him that she might have the *dassa*. But her bite had left no doubt in his mind as the mating bond spread through his system, connecting him to her at a molecular level. His need to strengthen that bond by sharing his own *dassa* was overpowering. It took every ounce of willpower to disengage, his thoughts muddy with lust. Part of him knew he needed to hide, but another, more primal part of him wanted to pound this interloper into the dust.

Instead, he froze in place, hardening his skin to mimic stone as Mae appeared in the doorway. "Did you know your statue's gone—Oh!"

Angie bolted from the bed. "Mae!" She sounded breathy and sexy as hell. "What are you doing here?"

The other woman half lifted a cleaning bucket, eyes locked on Sten. Her focus drifted downward to his very obvious erection. "Is that… Is that your gargoyle?"

Angie snatched some clothing from the floor. "He's… um…" She tripped over a pant leg as she tried to step into it, almost landing on her face. His muscles tensed with the instinct to protect her, to catch her if she fell. But she managed to get her jeans up around her waist and hurried to his side while pulling a shirt over her head.

"I…" she stammered again, then with a resigned sigh said, "Mae, I'd like you to meet Sten. Sten, say hello to my best friend, Mae."

Mae's gaze remained transfixed on his cock. He hadn't entered the *duramna*, only a shielded state that hardened his skin to imitate stone. But the shift had captured his erection, and it wouldn't dissipate until he shifted back to his fully mobile state.

Stepping in front of him, Angie wrapped the quilt around his waist. She looked into his eyes. "Cat's out of the bag, Sten. You can't hide now. Say hello."

Resignation settled over him and he looked toward Mae. "I recognize her."

"Then you know she's my friend."

Mae took a backward step through the doorway. "I should… come back later."

Sten surged forward, one hand wrapping around Mae's arm. "Wait."

Mae's eyes widened, and she shrieked.

Angie put a hand on Sten's arm. "Hey, slow down."

"She cannot leave," Sten said. "What if she tells the authorities?"

"She's not telling anyone." Angie turned back to her friend. "Right?"

Sten waited until Mae nodded before releasing her arm.

Angie took the bucket from her friend's trembling hand. "And you can't leave yet. Not until we talk. A lot has happened, as you can see. Let's all go downstairs." Her small hand slid into Sten's, sending a wave of possessiveness through him. His need to share his *dassa* with her was making it hard to think, despite the presence of the other female.

Leading him past Mae, Angie paused to say conspiratorially, "He's harmless, I promise. Probably just grumpy from low blood sugar."

Mae nodded, gaze still wide.

In the kitchen, he moved toward a cupboard, hunger driving him toward the delicious minerals of the brightly colored dishes she'd served him yesterday.

"Leave my dishes alone." Angie smacked his hand, ignoring his scowl. "Go sit." She pointed toward the table in the breakfast nook. "I'll have food for you in a minute."

The chair creaked loudly as Sten sat, stiffly holding the edge of the quilt to his waist. Mae headed for another cupboard and poured a generous amount of tawny liquor into a glass. After taking a large swallow, she poured another glass and set it beside the stove for Angie. She glanced toward a glowering Sten. "Does he drink?"

Angie shrugged. "I honestly don't know. Ask him."

Sten answered before Mae responded. "I have a fondness for wine."

Mae raised a brow in question toward Angie. "Have any wine?"

"Sorry, no. Just give him some tequila."

Mae poured him a glass and set it on the table in front of Sten. "I know I always joked he was your boyfriend, but this is crazy."

"I am no longer a boy. I am a man," Sten said.

"I think we've established that." Mae dropped her gaze to the quilt around his waist.

While nakedness didn't usually disturb him after so many years on this planet, he could sense it had an effect on this Earthian, and he was thankful for the covering. "Then what is a boyfriend?"

"A romantic partner." Mae quirked an eyebrow at her friend over her glass. Angie's skin had turned a deep pink.

Sten nodded in satisfaction and picked up the glass Mae'd given him. "I believe that is the correct term, then." He downed the tequila. His stomach was a pit of emptiness, and he considered taking a bite of the glass.

"No nutritional value in glass, Sten." Angie reminded him. She offered him an obscenely small pink sausage. "Eat this while I warm up the rest."

Mae wrinkled her nose. "You're feeding him hot dogs? Really?"

Angie flushed. "I stopped at the gas station on the walk home. It's not like they carry prime beef."

"What are hot dogs?" Sten asked, taking the link. "I have always avoided eating pets."

Mae's face paled. Angie just laughed. "As you should."

Sten took a tentative bite. It was soft and very salty, but had calories, and right now, he needed as many as he could get. He shoved the entire thing in his mouth. He should've sought food before letting himself be distracted by Angie's alluring scent. Now he was half-crazed with hunger in addition to her *dassa's* effects. Watching Angie cut up several more links and mix them into a dish of baked beans, he said, "I do not understand why Earthians consume such large amounts of sodium."

Mae gave Angie a withering look. "I can't believe you're feeding him those." Heading to the fridge, she pulled out a stick of butter and the carton of eggs. "These were laid fresh today."

His stomach growled loudly. "I have enjoyed eggs many times. We have them on my planet as well. They are a nutritious source of protein and calcium."

"Planet?" Mae gaped.

Angie took the eggs. "Go sit and I'll try to explain."

While his *Hondassa* talked, Sten ate another cold hot dog. Mae listened with wide-eyed attention as Angie explained how Sten had crashed on Earth and had been guarding the family for generations. She didn't mention her ancestry, however, for which he was grateful. Angie's blood-line was best left a secret.

As he finished the last bites of the food Angie gave him, Mae finished her tequila and leaned back in her chair, looking Sten over appreciatively. "So, you're her guardian come-to-life alien statue and now you're serving her in more ways than just as a bodyguard." She rubbed both eyes with her fists and shook her head. "Okay, I guess that explains everything. How are you going to explain this to Mrs. Hendricks when she asks about the missing statue? Or do you plan to go back to statue form now that Angie's no longer in trouble?"

Sten fastened his gaze on Angie. There was no going back to the way things had been, especially now that she'd claimed him. But unlike Graj in the early days, he didn't have a perception filter device to disguise himself as a human. "It would be best if we left this place. My commanding officer, Zaek, has a cabin in the mountains. We will stay with him until we acquire a home of our own—"

"Wait a minute. Just hold on there." Angie put her hands on her hips. "This is my home and I'm not going anywhere."

Mae chuckled. "This girl has roots growing out of the soles of her feet. She's got a college degree but is now working as a waitress in in the middle of nowhere. There's no ripping her off this piece of dirt."

Angie crossed her arms and frowned at her friend. "My home is not a piece of dirt."

Mae sighed. "You know what I mean."

Sten knew Angie was attached to this house. He actually liked that about her and enjoyed watching her make things grow. But he wanted to work by her side and build a home together; it would be impossible to do that if they remained among Earthians. "I cannot go back to being a statue now that we are mated."

Angie's face went pale. "Mated? Who said we were mated?"

He frowned and touched his shoulder where she'd claimed him earlier, although his rapid healing had easily covered up the mark left by her blunt teeth. "You did."

Shaking her head, Angie retrieved the bottle of tequila and poured herself a hefty splash. "Mae called you my boyfriend, not husband. Different things, Sten."

Mae stood up and pushed her chair in. "I'm going to take this turn in the convo as my cue to go home."

Sten shifted his gaze to Mae. "You will not tell anyone of me."

"Mum's the word, I promise." Mae stuck a hand in her pocket and fished out her keys, then paused to catch Angie's full attention. "You going to be okay?"

"Yes, thank you." Angie threw back the contents of her glass in a single gulp. "I'll see you in the morning."

Mae raised her eyebrows and pursed her lips, but nodded. Then she met Sten's gaze and said, "It's your job to keep her safe. Even from yourself. Remember that. Anything happens to her and I'm calling in a wrecking ball to level your ass. Got it?"

He nodded, which seemed to satisfy her. Once the front door shut, Sten moved his chair closer to Angie. "We need to discuss leaving. Remaining among Earthians is dangerous, especially now that you are my *Hondassa*—"

She twisted sharply to face him. "You said you would not give me the venom or whatever without my consent."

He felt his blood cool as he realized she didn't know what she'd done. "*You* bit *me*. A primitive way of claiming one's mate, but still…"

She let out a shaky breath. "I thought only males had the *dassa*."

"Females are just as capable of choosing mates as males. The bond is strongest when both mates share *dassa*. I will give you mine now if you'd like."

She held one palm out as if to stop him. "Hold on."

His chest felt empty as he realized what her reaction meant. "You do not wish to bond with me."

"I only just met you." She poured herself another shot then dropped her head into her hands. "I don't know what I'm feeling."

He cleared his throat. The fire of her *dassa* was burning through his blood, demanding reciprocation. Yet she knew little about him or his species, regardless of her heritage. He was a monster on her world. It'd been a miracle she'd wanted him in the first place. "If you do not wish to be my mate, I understand." Yet her rejection hurt like nothing he'd ever felt before. All he could think of was putting some distance between them. Immediately. "I will go."

Rising, he moved toward the parlor.

"Wait!" Her cry stopped him. "You can't just leave. I—I…"

He turned to find her on her feet, a look on her face that made him want to pick her up and carry her back upstairs to finish what Mae'd interrupted. But she was more human than Khargal, and her bite had not meant what he'd hoped. She had not intended to claim him. His chest ached, but he knew he needed to give her an out. "The mating is not permanent. Given time and distance, your *dassa* will dissipate from my body and our bond will subside." While technically true, Khargals who'd shared their *dassa* for a long time often couldn't survive the death of their mate. The amount of *dassa* she'd shared with him wouldn't be that strong, but he would most likely spend the next few decades in withdrawal. "It will be best if I leave you now."

"Give me time to think about this." She stepped forward and placed her hand on his bare chest. "Please?"

The warmth of her hand and the pleading in her eyes unraveled his resolve. He had intended to retreat to the hills overlooking her house and resume his watch; his duty to protect her only strengthened with the claiming. Remaining nearby would strain his willpower not to touch her, but he would try because she asked. "I will return to your garden for as long as I am able."

Without waiting for her to speak again, he retreated through the house, making sure to close the front door firmly behind him.

❦

Angie sat in stunned silence as Sten left the house. Mated? Was such a thing even possible for humans? Yet if Sten was telling the truth—and the longer she knew him, the more she believed he was—she wasn't completely human. And she couldn't deny the aching grip he seemed to have on her heart. The few boyfriends she'd had never made her feel like this, like they owned a piece of her soul and would take it with them if they left. She would be empty if Sten wasn't here. Was that an effect of the mating bond? What would it feel like if Sten strengthened it with his *dassa*?

In the pit of her stomach, she wanted to know. Wanted to feel that intensity.

Sally pushed in through the pet door at the back of the kitchen, her gray fur dusted with a pale sheen of pollen. She'd shown up in the garden one day about a year ago, thin and mangy, and Angie'd started feeding her out of pity. Now the cat sat next to her empty kibble dish and let out a plaintive meow.

"You said it, sister." Angie refilled the dish and then

plopped down in the nearby seat to watch Sally eat. The cat still didn't like to be touched, but she was a good mouser and nice company in the garden.

Though apparently she'd had more company than she'd realized all along. Regardless of whether she chose to complete the mating or not, he couldn't continue living in her garden. That wasn't any kind of life, no matter what he said about duty.

The lights over the breakfast nook made her eyes burn, and she lay her forehead against the cool Formica tabletop. She'd barely slept last night, and most of tonight was gone already. Perhaps she should sleep. Things would be clearer in the morning.

She trudged up the stairs to bed, shutting off lights as she went. Moonlight slanted in through her windows, and she looked down into the garden at the silvery shadows around Sten. She'd always looked with such pleasure at her garden, but now when she peered out, all she felt was longing deep in her gut. *Isn't that your answer?*

She pressed both palms to the glass, catching a glimpse of his glittering emerald eyes watching her from below. His pose was definitely different now. Tense. Pained. A reflection of her own emotions. She felt horrible, letting him stand out there alone in the dark. But he was a gargoyle. A living, breathing gargoyle. How could that even work? And how would she explain to the rest of the town why her statue was gone?

What if I sold him? Not really sold him, but pretended to. Although she'd told York the gargoyle was part of the historic property, that wasn't exactly true; the building was on the historical record, but the moveable items on the property were hers to do with as she pleased. All she'd need was a bill of sale, to borrow Mae's pickup so she could "move" him off the property, and Sten would be free.

Eyelids heavy, she realized she'd made up her mind. She wanted to complete the mating. She wanted Sten to stay with her even if it meant they holed up inside all day and only came out at night.

Smiling, she turned away from the window, stripped down to her panties, and climbed between the sheets. That would at least solve one problem. Now she just needed to come up with a way for him to pass as human.

❧ 8 ❧

Sten's *duramna* refused to settle over him. With Angie so close, he could not bear to shut himself off in the deep sleep. But it meant he was aware of every sound, every movement inside the house. He watched the mangy cat skulk around the corner of the house toward the backyard. Listened to the crickets sing to the moon. Breathed in the honey-almond perfume from the flowers Angie loved to grow beneath her bedroom window.

When he'd entered her room while she was showering, his hunger for her had been unbearable, more necessary to him than food. She did not feel the mating pull like he did. The aching hollow in his chest hurt as much as her unintended *dassa* burning within him. He glanced up at the stars. He'd been on Earth longer than he'd been alive on Duras, and tonight he found himself yearning more than ever for a rescue ship to take him home. To remove him from this temptation. If he went to her again, there would be no stopping his mating instinct. He would

62

fill her with his *dassa* as surely as he'd fill her with his seed, making her his in every way possible whether she wanted him or not. He should remove himself from this place immediately.

But there was no escape for him. His gaze returned to the house he'd watched for over a hundred years, imagining her lying naked on her sheets. As long as he was on Earth, he would keep Angie safe, whether she wanted him as a mate or not.

As the darkness of night passed into the gray light of morning, the front door opened and Angie darted out, once more dressed only in panties and tank top. He hardened his skin to keep his erection in check. What was she thinking? Was she trying to make this as painful as possible?

She headed straight for him, bare feet crushing the golden flowers surrounding him and filling the air with peppery perfume. Her pheromones intermingled with the flowers, musky and earthy, and his mating gland surged to life, filling his mouth and making his teeth ache.

He unfroze his lips enough to say, "Go away before I do something you regret."

She smiled at him and put both hands over his cheeks, eyes sparkling with excitement. "I want to be with you." Her words slammed into him like a meteor. "I have a plan, but need to get some things in order. I'll talk to you again after dark."

Then she darted away, gone again as fast as she'd arrived, the front door closing solidly behind her. Soon, the loud rumble of Mae's truck came to a stop at the gate behind him. Angie emerged from the house, pausing only long enough to kiss him before jumping into the truck.

Mae's voice floated from the open window. "I half expected you to have eloped last night."

As Angie closed the truck's door, he heard her say, "I need to borrow your truck."

They pulled away, making Mae's response unintelligible. Sten remained frozen in place, lips tingling from Angie's kiss. The Prime Directive forbade revealing oneself to species with lesser technology, and he'd become known not only to Angie, but to Mae. Yet they were taking his existence remarkably well. Had Earthians progressed enough to allow aliens to live among them? They might not yet be up to par with Khargal technology, but they might be ready for limited interaction. A pang of loss for Graj swept through him. The science officer would have been ecstatic to see the evolutionary changes in Earthian culture.

The mailman came and left, and the sun rounded its zenith while Sten maintained his watch. He allowed himself small adjustments of his head and eyes, taking note of details that would not register while in his *duramna*; the red globes of tomatoes hanging from their vines, the upturned faces of yellow sunflowers, the cherished pot of some herb he didn't know the name of on the corner of the porch. Angie's horticultural skills would be revered on Duras, where plant life struggled to survive even in the most temperate zones.

But that was not an option. This was her home. He saw her in every leaf and stem, in the peeling paint and the repaired roof. If he wanted her, he needed to make this his home, too, even if it meant cutting off his horns and tail to live among Earthians. Hopefully, it wouldn't come to that; he knew of at least two Khargals who owned perception filters that could disguise them to look like Earthians. He would reach out to them and see if they could help.

Angie returned that afternoon, arms loaded with brown paper bags. She leaned close to him and said, "Fried chicken tonight," before sashaying into the house.

Soon the mouth-watering scent of frying meat and spices reached him. He waited impatiently for darkness to conceal his absence, then drew himself up and headed inside.

Angie was on her hands and knees in the parlor, hands covered in pink rubber gloves and hair pulled back into her usual, messy bun. She looked over her shoulder at his entrance, then sat back on her heels. "The blood is never going to come out of the hardwood floor, let alone the carpet."

He took a step forward. "I will assist you."

She pulled the gloves off and stood. "We have more important things to do." She picked up a folded stack of clothing from the base of the stairs and held it out to him. "I didn't know if gargoyles wear clothes, but I pulled some of Dad's clothes out of the attic just in case you'd like something to wear."

"Thank you." It had been many centuries since he'd bothered with clothing. His crewman's uniform, designed to alter itself to accommodate his physical changes, had deteriorated long ago, and he'd found it easier to simply strike a modest pose during his years in his *duramna*. He retracted his wings and reached for a plaid button-down shirt.

Angie gasped. "Your wings! How did you do that?"

He smiled at her, turning to show her the slit along his shoulder blade. He forgot she hadn't seen him without his wings. "They retract."

She stepped closer and ran her fingertips along the slit. A

shiver ran through him at her touch. Shaking her head, she said, "Well, this is going to make hiding you a lot easier."

"It is still impossible for me to hide this." He gestured to his face.

"Oh, I don't know. The right hat, maybe a pair of sunglasses..." she teased.

"I do not believe that is possible."

"Spoilsport."

He sorted through the denim jeans and plaid shirts he'd been accustomed to seeing William wear for so many years. The man had been large, but not as large as Sten. Selecting a pair of jeans, he discovered a hole had already been cut for his tail. He shot a questioning look at Angie, who only grinned and shrugged. "Not like my Dad needs them any more. You might as well be comfortable."

"Thank you." He pulled them on. His ankles and clawed feet stuck out a little too far, but at least he was covered. Angie licked her bottom lip as she regarded him and his cock surged against the denim. His voice thickened as he asked, "Is this acceptable?"

"Um, yeah." The glazed look vanished from her face, and she turned away to lead him into the kitchen. The smell of meat and potatoes permeated the air, making his stomach growl. The table had already been set with dishes, so he sat while she brought over several serving platters. "I wanted to show you that I can cook—when I have food around."

"It smells delicious." He picked up a perfectly browned chicken thigh and bit into it, crunching through bone and all.

Her mouth dropped open in surprise, then she laughed. "Is there anything you won't eat?"

He regarded the juicy meat, realizing how very unhuman he must appear to her. Not the best way to attract an Earthian mate. He set the meat down. "You said you wished to talk."

"I have a plan to get you out of the garden without raising too many questions."

He held very still. This wasn't exactly what he had hoped to hear, but it was a start. "Go on."

She grinned. "I'm going to sell you."

He stiffened. "Did York approach you again?"

"No, but he gave me the idea." She picked up an ear of corn and rubbed butter on it. "I'll create a fake receipt and borrow Mae's truck to haul you off. I'll make sure to drive you through town so everyone sees."

He nodded. The plan made sense, and would work whether she wanted him to stay and be her mate or he retreated to the rocky hills. "That is good. Once the town knows I am gone, they will not continue asking questions."

"Mrs. Hendricks will pitch a fit, but at least she won't call the police again, thinking you're stolen or something." She set down her cob. "But that's only half of my plan. I don't think we can disguise you as a human, not under close scrutiny. But we could change our schedule around so we sleep during the day and spend time together at night. It's not ideal, but it would let us be together."

His throat tightened. He needed to hear her actually say it. "Are you asking me to be your mate?"

She flushed. "Only if you think you can live that way."

Now wasn't the time to tell her of the perception filter. Now was the time to make her his, now and for always. Every cell in his body surged with anticipation. "I would do anything to be with you."

Her smile seemed to light up the room. "Then I think we have some unfinished business."

They barely made it to the bedroom before he'd ripped the clothing from her body. Burying his face between her breasts, he inhaled her scent—his *Hondassa's* scent—and wrapped both arms around her to clutch her backside. She threaded her fingers into his hair and sighed. His cock was painfully hard, trapped against the fly of his jeans. His instinct told him to take her, hard and fast, to claim her as his now, before she changed her mind. But his heart wanted to take this slow. To savor her. To make his claiming a night she would cherish for the rest of her days.

He lay her back on the bed and slid his pants from his hips, struggling for a moment to free his tail. He got them off to find Angie watching with a hunger that rivaled any Khargal's. "This taste in my mouth. Salty and sweet. That's my *dassa*?" she asked.

He nodded, allowing her a moment to think about it. She ran her tongue along her front teeth as if savoring the flavor. Then she gestured to him. "Come here. I want to see what you taste like."

He stepped closer, and she leaned in to take his shaft into her mouth. The exquisite sensation of her lips enveloping him made him groan. His wings sprouted from his back, flexing to help him balance. His hands found their way to the back of her head, claws extending out of instinct as he encouraged her to take him deeper. Somehow, she opened to him, taking all of him then pulling back, her tongue circling his head before plunging forward once more. He flexed his hips, taking shallow breaths as she drew his erection to an almost painful hardness.

"*Lar*, you're killing me," he groaned.

She made a noise with her mouth still on him, the vibration an exquisite sensation. She slid her hands beneath her chin to fondle his balls, coaxing them from their usual place hidden tight against his body. One hand circled the base of his shaft, squeezing in rhythm to her sucking. His climax rose inside him while his *dassa* flooded his mouth. Suddenly, she sucked hard, and his orgasm surged from him in a wave.

He may have shouted. He didn't remember. All he knew was ecstasy.

Angie pulled away with a satisfied smile, wiping the corners of her mouth while Sten swayed at the edge of the bed, one hand on the corner post for support. His breathing couldn't catch up. She patted the mattress beside her. "Lie down."

Grateful to comply, he retracted his wings and flopped down on his back next to her. She leaned over and kissed him —he was becoming quite fond of this Earthian thing—and his hand found the softness of her breast. Her nipple hardened under his palm, and his cock twitched back to life. "How do you do this to me?" he asked, flipping her onto her back so he could stare down into her face.

"Must be the Khargal in me."

"I'll show you a Khargal in you." He thrust one knee between her legs, parting her so he could caress her lower lips. She was swollen and slick with need, and his finger found the sensitive bud between her folds. Working in circles, he flicked the sensitive area until she squirmed. Then he latched his mouth onto a nipple. She cried out, and he rubbed faster over her clit. He kept going as the rolling spasms of her orgasm subsided, then he brought his other knee in line with his first, positioning his cock at her opening.

She tilted upward, taking the head of his cock inside. He teased her with it, entering partially while he flicked her clit. Her opening tightened and her breath came in tiny, mewling pants. "Please."

"I would like to share my *dassa*." He knew it wasn't fair to ask now, when she was on the verge of climax, but he didn't think he could resist claiming her while giving her what she wanted.

"Yes, please. Just do it."

With a hard thrust, he entered her. Her heat coated him and she screamed in pleasure, bucking upward to meet him. His *dassa* filled his mouth, coated his teeth. He barely had time to remember a human's skin was more fragile than his own as he bit down on her shoulder.

The action seemed to spur her orgasm, her inner walls tightening rhythmically around him and driving him to his own climax. Spent and breathless, he collapsed, rolling to lie beside her, his mind an empty void except for one thing. He turned his gaze to Angie's flushed and glowing face. "*Hondassa.*"

9

From her spot on the porch, Angie strained her eyes across the dark garden to where Sten was lifting a rock that no man should have the strength to move alone, at least not without causing a hernia. Thunder clouds had rolled in that afternoon, and while no rain had fallen, the air smelled like ozone, and a stiff breeze was kicking across the ground. She was surprised Sten could see without a flashlight. "Be careful, there are daffodils planted around there. Are you sure you don't need a flashlight? "

"I will be cautious." He scratched at something in the dirt. "Ah, here it is." He glanced around the dark neighborhood and moved toward the house carrying a dirt-crusted box in both hands. He'd hidden his sigil inside who knew how many ages ago, and he expected it somehow to still work.

She wrinkled her nose, eyeing the box as he ascended the porch steps. "Burying it may not have been the best idea."

"Our sigils are designed to withstand time and elements." He passed her, entering the house.

She followed him and closed the door, securing the lock. Ever since the break in, she couldn't shake the creepy feeling she was being watched. "You have all this technological advancement, so why didn't you all come with disguise technology when you landed here in the first place?"

He furrowed his brows. "We did not land, we crashed. And perception filters were reserved for personnel who needed to infiltrate other cultures."

"And you think one of the other Khargals will give you theirs?"

Sten moved toward the kitchen. "I would not ask such a thing. But Felinray created a modified version using Earthian parts. My hope is he can duplicate another one for me."

"You said Grandpa Graj had one." She'd taken to calling her ancestor that as they talked about her history and the other Khargals. The way it rolled off her tongue made her smile, although Sten was not nearly as impressed. "What happened to it?"

"Destroyed in the fire along with his body." He set the small chest on her kitchen counter, face grim. "A preferable option to allowing Earthians to possess technology beyond what they have earned the right to wield."

She raised her eyebrows. "You hid your sigil under a rock. I don't think that's a very sure way to keep it out of human hands."

He smiled. "It is more secure than wearing it around your neck."

She touched her mother's pendant at her throat. "So, why didn't you take this one and hide it, too?"

"The sigils are linked. I can use one to track the location

of another, which has been useful over the generations when your family moved and I needed to follow them."

That reminded her of how much she still had to learn from and about him. He broke the box's seal with a claw, sending a scattering of dirt across the counter, and withdrew a ruby-colored sigil that matched the one she wore around her neck. Her gaze was drawn to the glint of gold in the bottom of the box.

She sucked in a breath. "Is that real gold?"

He jiggled the box, and she realized it held more than a handful of coins. "When your great grandfather began mining here, another human attempted to kill him. I was forced to exterminate the man." He picked up a coin and held it out to her. "These were on his body."

The twenty-dollar coin was date stamped 1895. It had to be worth a lot more than twenty dollars now. "That's been hidden under that rock since the house was built?"

"Yes. They are not edible. You may have them if you like."

"Really?" She grinned. "If I can get my broken window fixed, Mrs. Hendricks might forgive me for selling my statue."

Sten pressed a facet on the sigil's ruby surface, and a hologram appeared above its surface, bathing the kitchen in red light. Alien scribbles scrolled across the surface. "Once I locate their signals, I will place a call to Felinray and Alkor."

She leaned against his shoulder as he flipped through several screens. He showed her a few key symbols, explaining what they meant. "These sigils once allowed us to access the ship's databanks. Now they are little more than communication devices. But if a rescue ship ever arrives, our sigils are the only means for it to contact us." Sten tapped a few emblems and another screen appeared with several dots on what looked like a map. He spent a few minutes interacting with the screen, then spoke into the sigil in a guttural yet sibilant language. When he put the sigil down, his face was solemn. "My signal doesn't have the same urgency as one from a ship. If they are in *duramna*, they will not answer right away. Perhaps for decades."

Angie felt her shoulders slump. "Decades?"

"It is not so long." He stroked her hair. "Remember, as my *Hondassa*, you are likely to live longer than a normal human."

She sighed, picking up the red gem. Even with an extended lifespan, decades felt like forever. "Should we make it into a necklace like mine? So you can keep it close?"

He smiled at her and shook his head. "Much as I like keeping it close, it would be unwise of me to wear this in the open. I must hide it once more."

"But what if someone calls back?"

He tapped his temple. "I will receive an alert."

"Huh. You've got mail, alien style. Okay. We need to hide it and the gold, too, at least until I can get the coins appraised and sell them." She grinned at him. "My four-poster bed has a hollow post where I used to hide my allowance."

She led him upstairs and unscrewed the upper half of the bed post. She dropped the coins inside, and he placed the sigil on top. As she aligned the post back into position, he said, "This is an excellent location."

How many times had she squirreled things away there as a child? "I found this hiding spot when I was jumping on my bed and thought I'd broken it. I was sure I was going to get in so much trouble. But then I found a rolled-up dollar inside and asked my dad about it. He laughed so hard. He'd found it the same way as a kid."

Sten nodded. "I see why you love your items. Each thing has history for you."

She grinned, loving that he understood. Mae sometimes gave her a hard time for not throwing things out. A yawn gripped her, and she glanced at her bedside clock. "I'm going to be useless at work again tomorrow."

"I will return to the garden and allow you to sleep."

She put a hand on his forearm, hating to let him leave. "I can't wait until you can sleep in here with me without anyone wondering where you've gone."

The air seemed to heat, and he took a step to bring their bodies together. He looked down into her face, emerald eyes glinting. "I am not used to social interactions. Humans say goodbye with a kiss, do they not?"

She swallowed, all traces of sleepiness leaving her. "They also say hello that way."

He gave her a wicked grin and pulled her onto the bed.

⊗

Winston York the Third was going to be the hero. The statue was definitely a gargoyle, based on the now-missing statue and the outline of a man with wings he'd seen entering the house earlier. Now it appeared the woman who owned the house was engaged in a sexual relationship with the creature—at least, that would be his guess based on the noises coming from inside the house. The Syndicate had always suspected some gargoyles maintained human minions to help hide them in plain sight, but the discovery of a breeding pair would seal his career.

He peeked around the tumbled brick wall he'd been lurking behind. His supervisor had told him to maintain his distance, and although this wasn't the best hiding spot, it was out of the gargoyle's line of sight. He was certain the woman was unaware of his scrutiny; she was too caught up in her perverted love interest to notice York.

He glanced toward the heavy clouds, wondering when the rain would start. Why was Headquarters taking so long to send backup? He dialed his cell phone, glad his position here had coverage, and relayed what he'd just witnessed.

His supervisor let out a long sigh. "You were told not to approach the subject."

"I haven't alerted them to my presence," he said. *Not since the first day I discovered the gargoyle.* But Headquarters already knew about that. York lifted his binoculars again, trying to see through the house's front window. "I'm simply keeping an eye on things to be sure we don't lose this opportunity. I need a team behind me."

"Keep your distance. An agent will be there in the morning and you can go back to your vacation."

"This is my case," York said. No way was he going to hand over something as juicy as this to someone else.

"You're an analyst, York. Not trained for the field."

"Perhaps not. But I know more about this than anyone." He'd done his research, kissing up to that red-headed old lady and spending hours of his vacation poring over historic mining ledgers. The gargoyle had arrived with the Martin family in the late eighteen-hundreds. He'd need to go back east to ferret out the trail. "There are things even you can't dig up on the Internet."

A short pause, then a sigh. "You can stay and work with the agent. But you hang back and let him do his job. Understood?"

"Understood." He grinned into the darkness. As long as he got credit, he was happy to allow a field agent to handle the guns. But the gargoyle was his.

❦

The next morning, Mae helped Angie pretend to load Sten into the bed of the pickup and together they drove through town, gathering a lot of stares as they went. At the one and only stop light, Angie spotted Mrs. Hendricks a block away. The head of the Historical Society would be the most put out by the sale of the gargoyle, so Angie wanted to make sure there was no question about what had happened to it. "Turn down here. I want to make sure Mrs. Hendricks sees."

Mae nodded and did a slow turn, pulling up beside the matronly woman. Angie rolled down the window. "Hey, Mrs. Hendricks!"

"What on Earth are you doing with that statue?" Mrs. Hendricks gaped at the bed of the pickup where Sten was tangled in a net of tie-downs.

"Someone offered to buy him. I have enough money to fix the window now."

"But that statue has been here as long as the house!" The matron put a hand to her throat. "You can't sell it."

Angie feigned concern. "I thought you'd be happy the

house was getting fixed. The gargoyle never really fit in, anyway."

"Dear, the tourists love to see your garden as much as your house. That gargoyle, as you call it, is an important attraction."

"Too late now." Angie shrugged and made a regretful face. "They already paid."

Mrs. Hendricks pursed her lips and shook her head. "Was it Winston York? He came into the museum asking a lot of questions about the statue. I can talk to him about returning it. He seems like a sensible man."

"No, it was another buyer I'd been talking to before him." Angie smiled, but it felt plastic. "We'd better go before it gets too late. We have a long drive ahead of us."

"Where are you taking it?" Mrs. Hendricks's voice grew muffled as Angie rolled up the window.

"Drive," she muttered through a clenched smile, and Mae put the truck into gear.

As they rolled out of town, Angie let out a long sigh and prayed Mrs. Hendricks let the matter go instead of trying to track down the non-existent buyer. They drove into Bozeman, stopping at a couple of trucking companies to get quotes about shipping the statue, just to leave a trail in case Mrs. Hendricks pursued it. Then they headed south out of town. On an empty back road, they stopped to drop Sten off. The plan was for him to fly home under cover of darkness.

Angie and Mae loosened the tie-downs, and as soon as the last one was free, Sten broke from his pose, shrugging off the straps and leaping from the truck bed, gripping the blanket they'd used as padding around his waist. "That was a most uncomfortable form of transportation." He scraped up some dry dirt from beside the road and scrubbed his face with it. "The insects here do not leave a pleasant residue when they are crushed."

Angie cringed. She hadn't even considered insects when she'd helped tie Sten in. "Sorry! I should've turned you around so at least you weren't face-first." She grabbed the roll of paper towels Mae kept in the truck and dampened several with her water bottle before moving in to help him wipe off. "I didn't even think about it."

Mae leaned against her truck, arms crossed, and shook her head. "I still can't get over the fact that you're not really a statue. How long can you hold still like that?"

"In my *duramna*?" Sten leaned into Angie's touch as she scrubbed at a spot on his temple. "Centuries."

Mae made a choked noise. "How old are you?"

"I lost count after a thousand."

"*Years*?" Mae looked like she might faint. "Holy fuck."

Angie folded the paper towel and wiped at his ear. She'd never really considered that he was exponentially older than she was. What would happen when she grew old and died?

Sten's wings came around her, creating a cocoon of privacy as he lowered his head to kiss her. Still clutching the damp paper towel against his chest, she relaxed into his embrace. He loved her now, and that was all that mattered. How his embrace could feel like home, she had no idea, but it gave her the same satisfaction she felt in her garden. "I brought you a pair of pants if you want them."

The mention of pants seemed to heighten the awareness between them, and he hardened against her hip. "I will not be able to wear them and maintain my disguise. But I will take them for later."

Mae's voice carried past the muffling effect of his wings. "If you're stone, how do those wings work?"

In a rush of air, he spread them wide, but kept one arm around Angie, holding her in front of him. He grinned down at her, then without warning, leapt upward. Angie sucked in a breath, fingers scrabbling against his hard chest to find a hand-hold as her feet left the ground.

"Jesus!" Mae shouted.

He carried her up and over to the opposite side of the vehicle with ease. As he set her on her feet once more, Angie threw her head back and laughed. She'd only half-believed him when he said he could fly. Now she wanted to soar through the clouds in his arms.

He looked down into her face. "I have missed flying."

"I can see why!"

Mae gripped the edge of the truck bed, staring over it with an open mouth. "Okay, you've proved your point. I guess you'll be fine getting back to Angie's place on your own. Just keep above the radar. Or below it. Or whatever. Don't get shot down."

"I appreciate your concern. I will avoid populated areas," Sten reassured her.

Angie wrapped both arms around his waist. "I want to fly with you."

"No way," Mae said. "You know Mrs Hendricks is going to be knocking on your door as soon as my truck rolls back into town."

Angie scowled. Mae was right. And it wouldn't be fair to leave her friend to answer questions. "Fine." She squeezed his waist tighter. "But promise me we'll fly together soon."

"That would please me."

"All right, love birds. I have other things on my to-do list today, so we need to hit the road."

An emptiness settled into Angie's gut. She wasn't ready to part from Sten. "Are you going to be okay?"

"Do not worry for me. I have done this many times before."

With a lingering kiss, she pulled away and retrieved his pants before climbing into the truck. Sten moved away from the road, his skin shifting color as he hunkered down and created a shell with his wings. At a casual glance, he looked like any other boulder.

"Think he'll be okay there until nightfall?" Angie asked.

Mae stared out the window. "According to him, he'd be okay there for a hundred years." She started the truck and pulled away. "He might not be able to pass as human, but he sure makes a great addition to the rock garden."

Angie watched out the back window until she could no longer tell him apart from the surrounding stones.

❧ 10 ❧

ngie puttered around the house, cleaning, watering the garden, waiting for Sten's return. He wouldn't be able to take to the air until after dark, and she could hardly wait to have him back. *For good.* Who would've guessed her perfect match would literally be in her own front yard? Around sunset, she went upstairs and took a long bath, shaved, and dressed in her sexiest lingerie. She had no idea if Sten would appreciate it or not, but it made her feel good.

Standing at her window, she gazed down on her garden, feeling nostalgic about her missing gargoyle, but also already considering what she could plant there now. She'd always wanted to grow fruit trees, and some of the new dwarf cultivars might look great in place of the statue. Knowing she might have a few hours of waiting, she lay down across the bed to read one of her gardening magazines.

Around nine the doorbell rang. She frowned and glanced toward the window. Flashing police lights glittered through the leaded panes. *Oh, crap.* She shot to her feet. What could possibly drag the sheriff out at this time of night?

Grabbing her robe, she threw it over her lingerie and headed downstairs. At the door, Sheriff Rollands stood outside holding a piece of paper. His gaze flitted over Angie's robe. "Evening, Angie."

"It's a little later than evening, Sheriff." She eyed the uniformed deputy and a stranger in a dark suit standing behind the sheriff. "How can I help you?"

"I'm afraid I have to bring you in for questioning." He held out the paper. "This here's a search warrant. That blood on your floor's been linked to a dead man."

Angie felt the color drain from her face. *A dead man?* But Sten wasn't even human. "Impossible."

"Come along and we'll try to get this cleared up."

She took a step backward, heart yammering against her ribs. "No, I—I can't."

Sheriff Rollands handed the paper to the deputy behind him before reaching for the handcuffs at his belt. "Just cooperate. I don't like this any more than you do."

"Am I under arrest?"

"The handcuffs are just protocol. We'll get them off of you at the station."

Something about this felt really wrong, but she knew the sheriff; he'd get through this with as little effort as possible. She gestured to her short, terry-cloth bathrobe. "Can I at least get dressed?"

The man in the suit spoke. "Afraid not. Search warrant says you are not to remove anything from the premises."

"I'm in my freakin' bath robe!"

"Sorry, Angie." The sheriff's mouth was a tight line. "They've got a warrant."

"Who is they?" She scowled at the man in the suit.

"FBI." The man flashed some credentials she barely had time to glance at before the sheriff was cuffing her hands behind her back.

This had to be a mix-up. Sten's blood wasn't human, so she'd just keep to her story about the bear, and everything would be fine. She allowed the sheriff to guide her down the porch steps past the FBI guy, who watched her with calculating eyes that made her want to squirm. What if they were here because they'd discovered the blood was alien? Her stomach flipped.

At the sheriff's Bronco, she hesitated, eyes on the night sky. Where was Sten? What would he do if he came back to find her missing? Or worse, strange people in her house? The sheriff prodded her to duck her head and get inside.

Knowing resisting would only lead to more trouble, she tried to meet his eyes. Maybe he could be reasoned with. He'd been super easy to convince about the bear. But he shut the door firmly behind her, avoiding her gaze, and climbed into the driver's seat. Angie focused on breathing and watched the house's lights flick on one after another. Strangers were pawing through all her precious things.

She leaned forward as Rollands started the engine. "Don't I have the right to be present while they search? I have delicate stuff in there."

"Warrant gives them the right to search without your interference. They won't hurt your stuff." He pulled away, heading down the hill toward the highway.

"What about my rights?" Nobody even knew where she was going. "Can I make a phone call?"

"This is a federal case now. You'll have to wait until we reach the station."

As they sped away from New Turnbull toward the county sheriff's office, her heartbeat seemed to be trying to out-race the Bronco.

❧

Sten pumped his wings, speeding through the night at full speed. His muscles burned, unused to flight after so many years, but it felt good to have the wind against his face and air under his wings again. Avoiding the lights over the small pockets of civilization, he reached the mostly-abandoned town of Old Turnbull, flying over the burned-out buildings and husks of brickwork marking places that had once bustled with miners and their families. He hadn't seen the community from the air since before the wildfire in the first half of last century had destroyed most of the buildings. Angie's was the only house in the old town still occupied, and the warm glow of lights behind the leaded glass windows on the first floor beckoned him like a signal fire called shipwrecked men to the beach.

Two unfamiliar cars sat parked in the street near the house, and he slowed. One had law enforcement lights on its roof, but they were dark. The other was a nondescript dark van.

Pulse pounding, he fought the instinct to fold his wings and dive toward the house. Had the intruder returned while he was gone? He couldn't approach without being seen. He should have known the break-in was no random thing. He'd let his guard down, and now Angie might be in serious trouble.

He circled for over an hour, yet still whoever was inside showed no signs of leaving. Then a ping at his temple alerted him that his sigil was receiving a message. *Lar, now?* Did it have anything to do with these people inside Angie's house? How many were there? The bare, rocky mountainside offered no cover other than what Angie grew in her garden, so he couldn't land anywhere near enough to see inside. He dropped altitude, listening intently for any indication of what was going on, and continued circling. *What was happening?*

Eventually, two men exited. A man in a deputy uniform said, "See you back at the station, then." He got into his vehicle and pulled away.

The other man turned his pale face toward the sky, and Sten swerved toward the mountainside, trying to hide his outline against the solid mass of land rather than stars. After a brief scan, the man pulled out a flashlight and directed the beam across the flowers where Sten had stood for so many decades. Sten barely dared beat his wings. A cell phone rang, and the man's voice floated through the silent darkness as he moved to the van. "No sign of him." The man continued speaking as he got into the van and drove away.

Was that everyone? Was Angie still inside? Sten dove for the house, landing lightly near the back door to the kitchen. "Angie!" Passing open kitchen cupboards, he charged through the empty dining room to the parlor. The air was full of the residual scent of other people, the floor Angie'd swept once more littered with broken figurines and papers. "Angie?"

He reached the top of the stairs in three huge steps and

hurried to her bedroom. All was still and quiet. Her bedcovers had been tossed aside and drawers hung open. Even the pictures that had decorated her walls hung askew. The other Earthians' scent was everywhere. *Lar, they'd taken her.*

His sigil pinged him again. He wanted to scream at it to leave him alone. Finding Angie was his main concern. He spun the post open and retrieved the sigil, thrusting it into his pocket. If he hurried, he might be able to catch up to one of the vehicles.

He was downstairs again in moments and took to the air, scouring the roads for the deputy's vehicle or the van. They were long gone. He ground his teeth, frustrated that he hadn't chosen to pursue the vehicles. Of course they wouldn't leave Angie behind.

He had to track down those men, now. The deputy leaving the house had mentioned the police station, but Sten had no idea where that was. Plus, it wasn't as if he could march in there and take Angie. He needed help.

Turning back to New Turnbull, Sten scoured the streets for Mae's familiar truck, finally locating it in the driveway of one of the homes. She would know what to do. He swept in next to her vehicle and crouched in the shadows, listening in case someone had spotted him. The proximity of so many Earthians made his stony hide itch, but no one seemed to have noticed him. He crept onto Mae's covered porch and tried the door. Locked. Glancing over his shoulder for onlookers, he rang the bell, then rang it again for good measure.

Inside, he heard movement. The porch light came on, and he sprang backward, flattening himself against the siding around the corner. The door opened. Mae asked, "Who's there?"

"Extinguish your light," he said quietly.

"Sten?"

"Please."

The light went out, and he peeled away from the house, pushing past a gaping Mae. She closed the door. "Is everything all right?"

"Do you know how to locate your sheriff's office?"

Mae's mouth dropped open and she nodded slowly. "What happened?"

"When I returned to Angie's home, there were police outside, and she was not there."

"Fuck. Let me grab my phone." Mae ran up the stairs and returned a moment later, already speaking into the device. "But the police were just at her place and now she's not there." Mae looked at Sten and shrugged. "Okay, thank you." She lowered the phone. "They say she was released. The sheriff's probably bringing her home now."

He ran his claws through his hair. Angie was in danger. He knew it deep in his gut. "I am concerned for her well-being."

"I'll call her." Mae dialed, listening until Angie's voice-mail picked up. Shaking her head, she said, "She never keeps her phone on her, but I'm sure she's fine. My advice is to just go back to the house and wait."

Sten was good at waiting—he'd done it for centuries—but this was an entirely different situation. His sigil pinged him again. He clamped his hand over his pocket, suddenly frustrated with himself once more. He could use his sigil to track her down. He should have thought of it first instead of allowing panic to drive him. Opening the door, he stepped onto the porch. "I will find her."

Mae said, "Let me know when she gets home, please? I'll keep trying to call."

Pulling his sigil from his pocket, he launched himself into the air. Once he was above the town's lights, he activated the tracking interface. An urgent message overlaid the map, but it wasn't from Frelinray or Alkor like he expected. It was a message from the one place he'd never thought to hear from again.

Home.

At the county sheriff's office, Angie stepped out of the Bronco only to be shepherded toward the back end of a van. "What's going on?" she asked the man holding her arm.

He wore a suit much like the other FBI agent and ignored her question with a face as hard and unresponsive as stone.

Dragging her feet as the agent pulled her along, she looked over her shoulder. "Sheriff Rollands?"

Rollands pushed his hat back on his head. "Now, my understanding was you wanted to question her here."

His voice was muffled as the doors to the van closed and the vehicle lurched into motion. The man who'd dragged her into the van settled in on the bench next to her. Another sat on the bench across from her, the butt of a pistol prominent at his side. Cold sweat broke out over her entire body. She felt like she was in a spy thriller. One where girls like her didn't come out alive. "I haven't been given my rights, you know." She looked between the two men. "This is all illegal."

Both men just stared at her as if she wasn't speaking English. Sten's warning about the men hunting his kind had just become a stark reality. No wonder he'd been so worried Mae might tell the authorities. How was she going to escape? Sten had no idea where she was. The back end had no windows, so she couldn't see what direction they were going. And these men looked like they'd prefer to shoot her over telling her anything.

After a long, uncomfortable ride with her hands still cuffed behind her and her bathrobe gaping open, the van stopped. The back end opened, revealing the vast interior of some sort of warehouse. The man next to her once more grabbed her arm, pushing her from the van. She stumbled forward, half-supported by his grip, and walked between the towering rows of pallets to a sort of clearing where a chair had been chained to a support column.

"Sit," the man at her arm spoke for the first time. He half-shoved her onto the chair and reattached her cuffs to a bar on the chair's back.

Then she was alone, surrounded by pallets of who knew what. "Hello? Where am I?" Her pulse pounded in her ears. "Someone tell me what the hell's going on!"

After what felt like a long time, a familiar figure strolled from between two rows of pallets. Winston York the Third. He wore the same suit he'd been in when she'd seen him the first time, but his gaze on her was far less dismissive than it had been back in her garden. "Angie Martin. Thank you for coming in to speak with us."

Angie wriggled against her cuffed hands. "I didn't come in to speak with you. I'm supposed to be talking to the FBI or something."

"Forgive the ruse, but after you were so uncooperative, we had to resort to more drastic measures to get your attention."

"I'm not selling you the house." Angie glared at him, straining against her cuffs. "And the gargoyle is gone. So fuck off."

York clicked his tongue. "Such language." He stepped forward and used both hands to close her robe over her chest. "Your situation has proven to be far more interesting than I first imagined. Your clumsy and obvious attempt to dissuade me from my purpose only strengthened my conviction that this gargoyle is one of those we seek. Why else would you refuse my offer only to conveniently 'sell' it to an unknown buyer a few days later?"

Angie grimaced. He was right. It had been stupid of her to ignore Sten's warning. Now she might never see him again. "Why do you want it, anyway?"

"That's a complicated question. Who would have ever expected to find one of those creatures in the middle of nowhere Montana? I would say it ruined my vacation, but that would be a lie." He reached around her neck. She shied away, but his fingers deftly unclasped her mother's necklace. "Do you know what this is?"

Sten had warned her not to allow the pendant out of her possession, but how was she supposed to protect it in this situation? "It was my mother's. What does it have to do with any of this?"

York held the gem up in the harsh light of the warehouse, the red facets glinting between the silver wire. "Our tech team will be thrilled to get their hands on this." He tucked it into the inside pocket of his suit jacket, then let his gaze roam up and down her body in a way that wasn't sexual, but made her skin crawl just the same. "What I'm most curious about is you, however."

A man in a lab coat moved in and pulled up the sleeve of her bathrobe. The sharp scent of alcohol rose between them as he swabbed the crook of her elbow.

She tried to squirm away, but she was still cuffed to the chair. "You people are insane!"

"Hold still, please." Lab guy's grip was making her hand go numb. He seemed to be having trouble inserting the needle.

"People will come looking for me, you know," she said through her teeth while lab guy jabbed her again. She was still processing everything York had told her. "You can't get away with this."

"We know how to cover our tracks." York paced with his hands behind his back. "Your charred body will be found in the morning. Such a tragedy you neglected to turn off the stove before bed."

"M-my charred body?" She could hardly breathe. Did they plan to kill her after all?

"Well, not yours, but someone who will fill your grave."

Lab Guy finally seemed to locate a vein, and she flinched as the needle pierced her skin. A cold weight settled into her stomach. Sten had said there were people hunting his kind. *My kind.* Did York suspect she had Khargal blood? A burning sensation ran outward from the insertion and made her fingertips turn icy. "What are you injecting me with?"

"Calm down," York said in an oily tone. "We're just taking some blood."

She gritted her teeth. "You have the pendant. Just take it and let me go."

"You know, I was disappointed when my associate failed to obtain the pendant that first night. But if he had, I would've never learned about your relationship with that "statue" of yours. There have been theories about gargoyles taking mates among humans. But all our attempts to breed them have failed."

The air suddenly didn't want to enter Angie's lungs. "Breed?" she choked out.

York gave her a condescending smile. "I noticed there has been quite a lot of… entertainment… going on at your house lately. I was willing to wait and watch, but then you relocated your gargoyle." He sighed. "It is better this way, I suppose. Studying creatures in the wild is always risky."

They'd been spying on her and Sten this entire time? And now they wanted her to "breed?" Her throat felt too tight to speak as she considered the implications. They were definitely after a hybrid. What would they do when they figured out they already had one? *Sten, where are you?* She let out a shaky breath and jerked against her cuffs, ignoring the sting as Lab Guy pulled the needle free. He stuck a bandage on her and picked up his tray of vials, now filled with samples of her blood. "I should have some preliminary results in the next hour or so."

"Very good." York nodded. "The mobile unit should arrive soon along with a full team."

The iciness in Angie's fingers crept upward to envelop her entire body. "Mobile unit? What are you talking about? I demand you let me go immediately."

York only smiled coldly and strode out of sight through the stacks, leaving her alone with her fear.

S ten followed the sigil toward Angie's location. The call from the rescue ship continued to ping him, demanding an acknowledgment, but he didn't have the energy to even think about that. Every tenet of the Prime Directive was in jeopardy right now, but most of all, his *Hondassa* was in enemy hands.

He prayed to *Lar* they hadn't separated her from her sigil, or he'd never find her.

After about an hour of flying at full speed, the white dot on his matrix told him he'd reached the location of Angie's sigil. He floated on an air current above one of the larger Earthian cities, sure he must be visible against the heavy cloud layer reflecting the glow of the streetlights. The streets below were nowhere near as silent as New Turnbull this time of night, and he'd have to be careful in his approach. Angie's signal appeared to be coming from a commercial district, and he alighted on the steeple of an old church to refine the signal's tracking.

Her sigil appeared to be in a large warehouse one block over. He moved to the next building over and wove between the HVAC units dotting the rooftops to survey the front of the building. A box truck was parked in front of one of the two closed bay doors. A smaller access door to the left of the bays was clothed in darkness.

He'd been out of touch for a few centuries, but he would not underestimate Earthian weapons; Earthians had come a long way since the days of arrows and muskets. Simply charging in would be like handing himself over, along with the sigil he carried. He crouched, straining his eyes in the reflected orange light from a distant streetlamp.

A man with a sidearm at his belt stood in the shadows by the door. *Silly Earthians.* It had been a long while since he'd faced the Rose Syndicate, but it was obvious they still had no appreciation for a Khargal's enhanced senses. He'd expected far more guards at the very least. Perhaps they were concentrated inside the structure.

Taking to the air, he flew a three-sixty around the building, looking for other entrances. A huge fork lift was parked against another bay door in the back, almost touching the building in an obvious attempt to block the door. He'd need to gain access from the front. Which meant disabling the guard.

First things first. Dropping to the ground beside the building, he skulked over to an abandoned truck sitting on its rims and sliced through the fake leather bench seat with a claw. He tucked his sigil into the stuffing among the springs. Whether he made it out of this alive or not, he couldn't allow any more technology to fall into Syndicate hands.

Beside the truck lay a pile of broken bricks, so he picked up several and once more took to the air. He felt like a barbarian, throwing stones at men with guns, but he had no other options. They had Angie and were sure to figure out she was a hybrid. Then he'd be facing more than a single guard at the door.

A well-aimed brick dropped the man near the door with a thud. Sten pulled back his arm, ready with a second brick in case more guards appeared, but no one seemed to notice the fallen man. Opening his wings, he shot over to the door and opened it quietly, slipping inside what appeared to be an office. The small room was dark, lit only by the illumination coming through the small rectangular window between here and the main warehouse. He crept forward and peered through. Rows of shrink-wrapped pallets reached toward the ceiling, but there was no sign of activity. Why were there not more guards? He might be a mere junior communications officer, but even he could recognize a poorly executed plan.

Slipping into the warehouse, he intended to leap on top of one of the stacked pallets, but then he spotted the breaker box right next to the office door. *How fortunate.* Within moments, the entire warehouse was plunged into darkness too deep even for his enhanced vision. Not that he needed his vision. He launched into the air, clicking his tongue to echo locate and avoid bumping into the dangling light fixtures.

Someone shouted from the recesses between the towering pallets. Then he heard a more welcome voice. "Sten!" Angie's cry was accompanied by the sound of metal scraping metal.

Below, someone turned on a flashlight, and Sten knew he had only moments before he lost his advantage.

Angie cried again, "I'm here!"

Angling toward her voice, Sten dropped down between several shrink-wrapped pallets, his nose now telling him exactly where to locate his *Hondassa*. His hands touched her flesh just as several emergency lights ignited along the warehouse perimeter. Angie sat in a chair with her hands bound behind her. Her smile at the sight of him melted his heart, and he wanted to kiss her soundly, right then and there, but now wasn't the time. Reaching behind her, he twisted the metal chain between her handcuffs, snapping it in two.

Angie stood, adjusting her robe's sash. "I knew you'd come for me."

"We must escape immediately." He pulled her into his arms and once more took to the air.

From inside a transparent plastic medical tent at the far end of the warehouse, a man in a white coat emerged and pointed. "He's flying!"

A gunshot cracked the air, and Sten dodged left, alighting on a row of pallets that nearly touched the ceiling.

"Do not harm the woman!" Someone shouted. "She may be pregnant!"

Sten stiffened for just an instant, his gaze meeting Angie's. "Pregnant?"

Her eyes were wide and she shook her head in a confusion that matched his own.

Macero. Among Khargals, pregnancy was a rare thing, sometimes taking hundreds of years for couples to achieve. How could Angie be pregnant so quickly? He had to get her out of here.

He eyed one of the vents overhead. The opening was too small for his broad shoulders, but Angie should be able to slip through easily. "I will distract them while you exit through that vent," he whispered against her ear, one hand pointing upward. "There is a forklift parked against the back you should be able to climb down."

She gripped his arm with both hands. "I'm not leaving you here."

"You must. I stand a better chance fighting them off alone. I will meet you."

"Where?" A sob hitched her voice. "They know where I live."

His heart wanted to break, but this was no time for softness. He thought about the rescue ship, finally coming to Earth after over a thousand years. She had to reach it and get off this planet, with or without him. It was the only way to escape the Syndicate. "My sigil is hidden inside the seat of a derelict vehicle outside. Retrieve it and follow the map north. My people are waiting there. Whatever you do, do not return home."

From somewhere below, a man shouted, "They're on top of the pallets!"

Sten reached up and tore the vent cover free, then grabbed her hips. "Go, now."

She tried to argue, but he hoisted her over his head, stretching his hardened wings to shield her from any stray bullets. More shouting came from below, and the warehouse echoed with gunshots. Although he'd hardened his skin, something penetrated his flank, and a wave of dizziness weakened his muscles. His hands slipped free of Angie's hips and he felt himself go numb as he toppled sideways.

Angie screamed, dangling from the vent by both arms.

Unable to control his wings, he plummeted toward the floor.

"Angie!" he roared. He hit the concrete flat on his back.

One wing made a sickening popping sound, sending stars across his vision.

Overhead, Angie's hands slipped from the vent opening. As if in slow motion, she tumbled toward him.

He had to save her. He had to move. To catch her. To stop her before—

She hit the concrete next to him with a sickening thud.

Sten's entire world seemed to stop on its axis. What had just happened? He didn't have enough control over his body to turn his head, and blackness pressed against the edges of his vision. From the corner of his eye, he gazed upon his *Hondassa*—his beautiful, broken *Hondassa*.

And then everything faded to black.

❧ 13 ❧

Angie kept her eyes squeezed shut and sucked in a shuddering breath. Was she dead? Every bone in her body felt bruised. *But not broken*—not that she knew what a broken bone felt like. She'd never sustained a significant injury in her life. But she imagined her bones should be broken in a hundred places from a fall like that. She should at the very least be in blinding pain.

Instead, the icy sensation she'd felt during Lab Guy's blood draw seemed to fill her bones and her skin prickled like static electricity raced across it. It hurt enough to bring tears to her eyes, but instinct told her the sensation was not harmful. It was more like the way growing pains used to feel when she was a kid. She listened to the men talking around her.

"When is the equipment arriving? I need x-rays." That sounded like Lab Guy.

"Thunderstorms are keeping flights from coming in. I told you we should have waited."

"Secure her." That was York. "I don't want her escaping."

"I'd advise against anything except a backboard," Lab Guy said. "If she vomits we need to be able to turn her. Besides, a fall like that breaks bones. She's not getting up anytime soon."

"What about the baby?" York asked, and she had to force herself not to reach for her belly.

Was she really pregnant? Or were they mistaking her hybrid DNA for pregnancy? Either way, she knew these men would never let her go. Letting them believe she was unconscious might be her only advantage at the moment.

"I can't tell you anything without equipment," Lab guy was saying. "We don't even know how far along she is yet. Are you certain she wasn't hit with one of the darts? I need to administer the antidote right away if she was. The dose is too much for someone her size."

"I don't know, Sir."

A frustrated sigh. "Take another blood sample and figure it out. Right now I need to deal with the creature. I want every pair of handcuffs in our possession on him until the rest of our equipment arrives."

Sten! They were talking about Sten. Keeping her eyes closed was one of the hardest things she'd ever had to do. Was he okay? She consoled herself with the thought that if they were talking about restraining him, that meant he was still alive.

"How long will the sedative from the dart keep him under?" The voices moved away and she felt someone slide a backboard under her. How many men were left with her? She waited until she felt herself being carried before cracking one eye barely open.

They moved her between the towering rows and into a brightly lit area surrounded in clear plastic, like one of those sterile tents on TV shows. A table with a microscope and other lab equipment sat on the far end. She sealed her eye shut as they set her on an exam table.

"You need me for anything else?"

Lab Guy's voice replied, "I've got it from here. Go help with the alien."

She listened to retreating footsteps while fingers prodded the crook of her elbow. Cracking one eye again, she saw Lab Guy bent over her arm with a needle. If she was going to do anything, now might be her best chance. Whipping her free arm up, she balled her fist and drove it against his temple with a sickening crack.

He crumpled to the floor. While he was still writhing, she swung her feet around and slid off the table. The medical tray next to her held a pair of handcuffs, so she grabbed them and yanked his arms behind him. She bound his ankles with the rubber tubing he'd looped around her upper arm. He groaned, and she knew all it would take was a cry for assistance and she'd lose her advantage. She snatched some cotton balls off the medical tray and stuffed them into his mouth before strapping a piece of tape across his lips. Not bad for her first tie-up job. Hopefully, it would be her last.

She stood and looked at her fist, expecting mangled fingers, bloody knuckles. Her hand was unmarred, but her skin looked gray. Stone-like. *Sten-like*. She let out a breath of a laugh. Had she just made her fist into stone? Was that how she'd survived the fall? She looked down at the rest of her below the hem of her gaping robe, but her skin looked normal and pink. She didn't have time for self-contemplation, however. Feeling naked in nothing but her lingerie and robe, she tightened her sash and looked around the tent.

The butt of a pistol hung part way out of the pocket of Lab Guy's coat. It looked a little different from the handguns she'd used in the past, and when she pulled the magazine, she saw three tiny darts instead of bullets. She transferred it to the pocket of her robe, regretting not stealing his lab coat before cuffing him.

Glancing around the sparse lab, she found a scalpel and tucked that into her other pocket. Whether she could shift her fist to stone or not, she didn't want to go face the rest of these men without weapons. Then she picked up a syringe filled with a clear liquid from the tray. It must be the antidote they were talking about. She didn't need it, but they'd said Sten had been hit with a dart. The antidote might be useful if she found him.

As she left the lab area, she glanced toward the ceiling. Had she survived that fall unscathed because she'd shifted to stone? Or had she healed like Sten had that first night she'd shot him? It didn't really matter. It seemed as if her Khargal heritage was finally emerging. What else might she be able to do?

Voices came from somewhere deeper in the warehouse, and she moved cautiously down the row toward them. Nearing the end of a line of pallets, she peered around the edge to find one of the men in suits talking to York. "—sure you're demoted to data entry by the time this is over."

York sneered at him. "You were in charge of firepower in this operation."

At the men's feet, Sten lay on his belly, hands cuffed

behind him and wings bound to his torso with multiple coils of rope. Angie sucked in a breath and pulled back so she wouldn't be seen.

The agent's voice could be heard from around the corner. "Operation? This isn't an operation, it's a complete fuck up. We don't even have a full team, and that storm's keeping air traffic grounded. If this thing wakes up, ropes and handcuffs aren't going to hold him. I don't know what they were thinking letting you loose in the field."

"I requested backup days ago and they sent me you. Even when I warned them the gargoyle was on the move. I've analyzed enough cases to know when we're about to lose a lead."

The agent's voice became a mutter that Angie had to strain to hear. "You hired people outside of the organization, and now not only do we have to create a cover up for the woman you abducted, but that guard at the door is dead. That's not going to be cheap or easily swept under the rug."

"It will all be worth it in the end." York was all but crowing. "We've put our hands on the trifecta the Syndicate has been looking for since its inception. A living alien specimen, his technology, and a female carrying his hybrid spawn. We're going to go down in history."

Angie felt sick. Her hand slid to the gun in her pocket. She had three shots, but she only needed two, right? Taking a deep breath, she prepared to swing around the corner.

Someone shouted from down the row behind her. "Hey!"

She spun, gun ready, and squeezed off a round at a man running toward her. The missile flew true, sinking into the man's shoulder. He made a gargling sound and sank to his knees. Behind her she heard York and the agent's footsteps approaching at a run. She whirled again, coming face-to face with the agent.

His teeth were bared, and he knocked the gun aside. It clattered to the floor. He reached for her.

Angie screamed, more of a war cry than fear, and ducked beneath his grasp. He seemed surprised when she dove into him instead of trying to get away. She slammed into his belly, sending a whoosh of air from him.

Tripping backward under her attack, he collided with York, who was right on his heels. York let out a startled cry, hands flying out. All three of them tumbled to the concrete floor, the men grappling for her. She squirmed free of the agent, only to have her head yanked back by the hair. York shouted, "Don't let her get away!"

"Sten, wake up!" she screamed, twisting against York's grip. "Sten!"

"Is that what you call him?" York twisted her head hard to one side and pressed her face against the concrete.

"Get off me." She drove an elbow into his gut and rolled to one side.

The agent had gotten to his feet, pulling his gun out and pointing it down at her. Thunder rumbled outside. "Don't make me shoot you."

She laughed, heart hammering as she stared down the barrel only a few feet from her face. "You won't shoot me. Not if you want this baby to live."

Once more baring his teeth, the agent swung the gun away from her—toward Sten. Keeping his eyes locked with hers, he said, "Then don't make me shoot him."

She'd been calling his bluff when he'd pointed the gun at her. Now it was her turn to bluff. "Go ahead. I already shot him once. He's bullet proof."

The man's face twitched with indecision.

That was all she needed. She kicked him in the kneecap, willing her foot to be as strong as her fist had been.

The crack of bone filled the air and he let out a strangled cry. "You bitch!"

Instead of falling away from her, he collapsed on top of her, pinning both arms around her thighs. *Shit!* She hadn't expected that.

York pounced again, wrestling her hands up over her head. The agent belly-crawled up her body, holding her down with his weight while his hands pinned her arms. "Go take a pair of cuffs off that gargoyle so we can secure her."

"Is that wise?" York sat back on his heels. "You said he could break free even with his current bindings."

Angie struggled uselessly. This guy was heavier than he looked.

"Secure the female and we'll use her as leverage if he wakes up." The agent's breath smelled like stale coffee.

Desperate, she clamped her teeth onto his shoulder, wishing she'd developed a Khargal's canines. She couldn't break through his suit's fabric, but he shouted and tightened his hold. "You're going to pay for that."

An explosion of movement erupted near York. Angie released her jaw and turned her head as York fell back. Sten had risen, wings shuddering and claws extended. His emerald eyes gleamed as his gaze met hers.

Ignoring the fallen York, he reached her in a single bound.

"Don't come any closer." The agent grabbed her throat with both hands. "I'll strangle her."

Her hands flew to his, trying to pry him free. For the briefest moment, her airway cut off. Then Sten ripped the man free. One handed, he flung the guy into the nearby row of pallets. The impact rocked the stack, and for a moment Angie feared it might collapse and bury them all.

She scrambled to her knees, spotting her gun on the floor a few feet away. As she lunged for it, she saw York rise, wielding his own gun.

"Sten, behind you!" she shouted.

Sten spun, but it was too late.

York fired. Sten shuddered and collapsed to one knee. A deafening roar escaped him. He reached for York. His frame shuddered and he toppled sideways.

"No!" Angie brought her own gun up and squeezed the trigger. York's mouth formed a perfect circle as he gargled something that might have been an attempt at speech. Body stiff as a board, he tipped forward onto his face.

Angie rushed to Sten's side. His eyes were closed, but he was breathing. "Sten?"

The agent made a sound, and she looked over her shoulder to find him on his belly clawing his way toward his gun. Gritting her teeth, she darted over to where York had dropped his weapon and fired a dart into the agent's backside. He wilted against the concrete. Part of her wished the gun had real bullets.

Dropping to Sten's side, she shook him, expecting his usual stony exterior, but his flesh was warm and pliable. Definitely not the *duramna*. Grabbing both of his arms, she tried to drag him. They had to get out of this warehouse before backup arrived. But even moving him a few inches left her breathless. He might not be stone, but he was still too heavy for her to move.

"Sten, wake up!" She smacked his cheek, breathing hard from her efforts. No response. She had to find a way to get him out of here.

Rising, she scoured the immediate area. Rain beat a heavy staccato against the roof, echoing through the vast building. Certainly a warehouse had handcarts or something? All she could see were pallets. She looked down into her mate's face. "I'll be back."

Dashing toward the lab, she skidded to a halt, scanning the warehouse for something to use. Lab Guy still lay bound on the floor, eyes closed. Somewhere in the distance, a siren wailed, and her heart skipped a beat.

Then she remembered the syringe in her pocket. She fumbled it free, staring at the clear liquid inside. It wasn't labeled, but she assumed the antidote. What if she was wrong? Kneeling by Lab Guy, she shook him, but he was unresponsive. *Dammit.* A tiny refrigerator sat on the table next to the microscope. She opened it, but the bottles and vials inside meant nothing to her.

Was the siren drawing closer? She darted toward the door of the nearby office. No handcart. Not even a rolling chair.

She let out a frustrated scream, then spun and ran down the other side of the warehouse, eyes peeled for a forklift or cart or even a skateboard. Anything that might help her move Sten. By the time she'd made a full circle and stood next to Sten once more, she knew she was out of options. She could hardly catch her breath past the stitch in her side. As she pulled the cap off the needle, her ragged breathing became a sob.

"Please don't die," she whispered, and jabbed the needle into Sten's arm.

⚜

Sten jolted awake.

Angie was pressing kisses against his forehead. Her face was wet with tears. "Oh, God," she kept repeating. "Oh, God."

He reached up and touched her cheek, unable to believe he wasn't dreaming. He'd seen her hit the floor. Had been sure he'd never see his beautiful mate again. "How are you alive?"

"We don't have time to talk. More of them are on the way." She grabbed his arm and tugged until he sat up. "Can you walk?"

Whatever tranquilizer had been in that dart was powerful. He felt drunk, but wavered to his feet.

"Do you feel okay?" She ducked under his arm to support him. "They talked about an antidote, but I wasn't sure what that injection would do to you."

"I will be fine," he said, despite the way he was having trouble focusing. His gaze swept the two men on the concrete. "Is this all of them?"

"There are two more through there." She pointed past the stacks. "York said something about not having a full team yet."

"Fortunate." He took a wobbling step, regaining his equilibrium as she guided him. His wings hung numbly against his back, and he didn't have the strength to retract them. "I must get you away from here immediately. Especially if you are with child." He'd believed finding his *Hondassa* was the ultimate gift; the thought of a family, of fledglings of his own, gave him new strength.

"You don't really think I could be pregnant, do you?"

He gave her a sideways smile. "The fecundity of your species has always amazed me."

"Could they just be mistaking my hybrid DNA for a pregnancy?"

"I do not know enough about the tests to judge, but I suppose that is possible." His chest tightened, surprising him. He would be disappointed if the test had been a mistake. "Either way, I must get you out of danger. Last night I received word that my people have sent a rescue ship. We will go back to Duras where it will be safe."

"D-duras?" She paused. "Leave Earth?"

He turned to her, taking her face between his palms. He knew how much her home meant to her, and now he was telling her she needed to leave it and her entire planet behind. "I am sorry, my love. You will never be safe here. Not with men like these after you."

"Is the ship here now?"

"Not yet, but soon."

She nodded mutely. He could tell she was trying her best to be brave, and he wanted to talk to her about it, but now wasn't the time.

They continued to the exit and he pushed open the door to peer into sheets of water falling from the sky. The smell of ozone and wet pavement wafted inside. "I hid my sigil inside the seat cushion of a nearby vehicle. We must retrieve it before we go."

"Oh, no! The sigil! They took mine." Without warning, she turned back and disappeared between the row of pallets.

"Angie, wait!" Sten careened into one of the stacks in his unsteady pursuit of her, wing cramping. "You don't need it."

Angie had already dropped to her knees next to York and was rummaging through his pockets. Thankfully, both men remained prone and unmoving. "What about your Prime Directive?"

"Any sigils left behind when the rescue ship teleports us onboard will self-destruct to prevent them from falling into the wrong hands."

"Doesn't matter now. I got it." She held the red-faceted necklace up. "Let's go!"

A wave of vertigo rocked him, and he had to pause and lean against a pallet.

"What is it?" Angie hurried to his side, once more placing his arm over her shoulders.

"I believe the drug they gave me is still having an effect." He closed his eyes and took a deep breath. This was no time for weakness. Not when his *Hondassa* was in danger. "I will be fine. Proceed."

They wove back toward the office and exited into the driving rain. Lightning flashed somewhere in the east, and a few moments later, thunder rolled through the air. Somewhere on the next block, a truck's backup signal beeped. Although the sky was still dark, morning was upon them, and the city was awakening. They had to get far away from here.

Sten took Angie in his arms and extended his wings.

White-hot pain lanced through him. He stumbled forward, nearly tripping.

Her feet backpedaled as his weight slammed into her. She let out a sharp breath. "What is it?"

Sten tested his wing again, realizing why he'd felt so numb. "I believe my wing is dislocated. I cannot fly."

14

At every intersection, Angie peered around the corner of the building, praying for no traffic while they crossed to the next block. Sten was not only injured, he couldn't retract his wings to hide them. They had to find a place for him to rest and heal. At least the downpour and the early morning light made it more difficult for people to see them, even if it made walking miserable. Her robe hung against her shoulders in irritating folds and stuck to her thighs, reminding her of how naked she was. If Sten didn't attract attention, then she surely would.

A truck rumbled along between the warehouses several blocks away, and she held her breath until it passed. Checking behind her to make sure he followed, she said, "Come on."

They managed to avoid detection until a bay door rolled open, spilling bright yellow light onto the drenched asphalt along with the voices of two bantering men. Angie yanked Sten toward a tiny church nestled between the warehouses, a remnant of some long-ago era when this land had probably been nothing more than a mining camp. "In here."

The door was locked, but Sten forced it open with a shove. They ducked inside, leaning against the door behind them. Angie's gaze darted around the tiny foyer. *God, please let it be the pastor's day off.* The church smelled like cleaning products and wood oil, and the dark wood paneling and decorative scrollwork had been well maintained.

A nearby coat rack held several bright yellow choir robes, and coffee supplies sat waiting on a folding table next to the sanctuary door. She scanned the bulletin board, hoping to learn the church's office hours. Almost buried beneath the community service announcements and a huge flyer for the upcoming Fall Festival, she spotted a little plaque with the church's office hours. She breathed a sigh of relief. "It looks like we have a few hours. The office doesn't open until ten."

Sten moved toward the sanctuary. "Still, we must seek seclusion."

Angie's stomach rumbled, and she eyed the coffee urn with longing. Any chance it might be full? Her insides were gnawing at her in a way she'd never experienced before, and while coffee wouldn't exactly fill her up, it would be better than nothing. She toggled the spigot as they passed, but it was empty. Pausing only long enough to tear open several packets of dry coffee creamer and upend them into her mouth, she hurried after Sten, who was already halfway down the aisle between the pews. The creamer did little to stop the biting ache taking over her middle. Why was she so unbearably hungry?

A side door behind the altar led to a small office with a

tiny window looking into an alley. Sten peered around the dim interior. "This is satisfactory for now."

She took off her soaked bathrobe, flexing her shoulders as she wrung it out. She felt like her entire body had turned into a prune in the rain, the itching, tingling sensation she'd felt since the fall still rippling over her in sporadic waves. Although her skin was covered in goosebumps, she felt strangely warm, as if whatever changes were happening inside her were heating her blood. She hung the robe on the back of the desk chair. "How long do you need to heal? Can I do something to help?"

Teeth bared, he stretched his injured wing forward and attempted to grasp the clawed tip. "I am afraid I will not heal on my own from this. And I cannot achieve the correct angle to readjust the joint on my own."

She'd never had to deal with an injury like this, but she'd seen a few movies where the hero had suffered a dislocated shoulder. Was a wing similar? "What can I do?"

He turned around. "You must pull hard enough to move the joint back into place."

Apparently it was the same as the movies. This was going to hurt like hell. Taking a deep breath, she gripped the end of his wing just above the claw. It felt more fragile than she expected, the membrane like buttery-soft buckskin. What if she did it wrong? Was it possible she'd do more harm than good? She swallowed, knowing she had no other option but to try.

While he braced himself, she pulled, but her hands slipped. Her mouth was filling with the salty-sweet flavor of her *dassa,* but she pushed it aside. How could she even be thinking about sex at a time like this? But the feel of Sten's skin was making her pussy tighten with desire.

He grunted and adjusted. "Again."

Where was her super-Khargal strength when she needed it? Or had she only imagined it when she'd punched the lab guy in the face? Summoning all her will, she tried again. No success. But Sten turned to her, his emerald eyes gleaming. "You are driving me crazy, *Hondassa*."

She licked her lips, trying to keep her gaze on his face and not his rippling abs. "I don't think I'm strong enough."

"Not that." His nostrils flared. "I can smell your arousal. It is distracting."

Her glance slid down to his waist, and she gulped. His cock was bulging against the fly of his wet jeans, actually moving as if it had a life of its own. "I can't help it. What's wrong with me?"

He took a step forward that in any other situation would've been menacing, but right now felt like a promise. "Unfulfilled lust can interfere with Khargal healing."

She licked her lips. "We're in a church. The pastor could come back at any moment. Or the Syndicate."

He flexed his hips. "Then we must be quick."

In another step, he was against her, his arms circling her waist. She arched into him, looping both arms around his neck and lifting her face to his kiss. His tongue slid along her lower lip, turning the heat between her legs into an inferno of need. One big hand flattened against her lower back, then slid lower to cup her ass before delving lower, until his fingertips met her pussy, probing against the fabric. Against her belly, his erection throbbed insistently as his tongue probed her. She opened her mouth wider, tangling her tongue against his, tasting her *dassa* mixing with his in an elixir more potent than any aphrodisiac on Earth or any other planet.

She dragged her hands down his front to open the robe. The crotch of his jeans bulged, straining the zipper, and the moment she'd released the button, the tip of his cock appeared above the waistline. Fuck, he was huge, and she loved every inch of him. She shimmied out of her panties while he jerked his fly the rest of the way open. Lifting one leg up around his waist, she pressed herself against him, rolling her clit over his hard length. "God, that's good."

He growled low in his throat and carried her two steps to press her back against the closed office door. The rough wood scraped her shoulder blades, and she wriggled finding a slight relief to the itch that had consumed her since her fall. Sten's wings shuddered behind him and he grunted, but kept his hold. Whatever pain he was feeling didn't seem to diminish his hunger. With both hands under her ass, he picked her up, impaling her with a single plunge. She moaned, throwing her head back and reveling in the fullness while clenching and unclenching her muscles around him.

Pulling back, he looked into her eyes and began driving into her, each ridge along his shaft stroking her most sensitive inner spots. Every slam drove her against the door, and she clawed her fingertips into his shoulders, gritting her teeth as wave upon wave of pleasure rose within her. Never had sex been like this before. Her body burned. She hooked her heels around him and strained to meet his thrusts. As she crested the wave of her climax, her spine stiffened. Something inside her seemed ready to break loose. She couldn't catch her breath. But she couldn't stop the momentum. Her orgasm rocketed through her, rolling up her spine and across her shoulders until she felt as if her heart might explode. She clung to Sten as if her life depended on it, feeling his return release fill her.

After a moment of heavy breathing together, Sten pulled back to look into her eyes. His mouth was slightly open, and a look of pride swept over his face. "My *Hondassa*."

She smiled languidly in return. He lowered her back to her feet. Her legs felt like rubber bands, but her shoulder blades burned, and another sensation reached her, something altogether unfamiliar. She turned her head to the right and yelped.

A delicate claw-tipped wing trembled against the door-frame. *Her* claw-wiped wing. "Is that... is that a fucking wing?"

Sten reached out and gently stroked the pinion. The sensation of his touch rolled through her. "Remember how we discussed my *dassa*, and that it would likely strengthen you and extend your life? It has also apparently strengthened your latent Khargal attributes."

"But wings? I mean, where did they come from?"

He reached beneath her arms and touched her shoulder blades where the wings emerged. "I imagine they have always been there. You just did not know how to extend them." He leaned in and kissed her before closing his fly. "Have I mentioned I like your underclothing?"

How was he taking this so well? This was freaky as hell, even if it was kind of cool. *Wings!* Did this mean she would be able to fly? She stepped away from the door and looked over her shoulder at the trembling wing tip. She concentrated and was delighted to watch it spread wide, fanning the air strongly enough to force her to reestablish her footing. "So, does this mean I can fly? Maybe I can fly us where we need to go."

Sten shook his head. "No, my little *Hondassa*. Learning to fly takes time. For now, you need to learn to retract them."

"Oh." She blinked at the outstretched pinion. With concentration, she could make it fan the air, but hell if she knew how to fold it up and make it disappear. "How am I supposed to do that?"

A crash from the alley outside made her jump, and she realized the garbage truck was here for pick up. Fuck, what time was it? She had to figure this out, or they'd never get out of here. Sten once more reached around her and placed his fingertips on her shoulder blades. The sensation of his touch against the base of her wings made her giggle. He chuckled. "Ticklish, huh? I'll have to remember that." Turning serious, he gripped the joint where it emerged from her back. "You must focus on retracting from here, not the wing itself."

That made sense. Angie closed her eyes, focusing on the spot his fingers had touched. A strange curling sensation rolled through her, making her insides clench. She gasped and reached out to steady herself, finding Sten's solid chest a welcome comfort. "Did I do it?"

He flattened his hands against her shoulder blades. "Well done. Now just remember not to let them unfurl on instinct."

"Great." Still unsteady from both her orgasm and the revelation she had wings, she picked up her panties and stepped into them. "So how are we going to get out of here if we can't fly?"

He let out a long breath. "We must continue our journey on foot."

On foot? "On foot isn't really an option. You stick out like a sore thumb." She glanced around the office again, hoping for a miraculous set of keys to the church van or something.

Her gaze fell on the office phone. "I think we should call Mae for help."

His brows drew together. "That would be unwise."

"I doubt they're watching her. York said he was short-handed, and he believed he'd already captured you." She picked up the phone. Calling Mae would be the smartest thing they could do. "She's a doctor—a nurse practitioner. I bet she'll know how to fix your wing."

He rubbed his jaw. "If you do not believe she is being watched, then it is worth a try."

Sighing with relief, Angie dialed. Mae picked up on the first ring. "Mae, it's me."

"Oh, thank God! Sten came looking for you last night—"

"I need your help. We have people after us and Sten's hurt." That last part emerged half choked as reality hit her in the gut. She would never see her house or garden again. Letting out a shaky breath, she gave Mae the address off the church's letterhead. "Would you also please bring me some clothes? And whatever you do, make sure no one follows you."

"Of course. Give me an hour."

"Thank you, Mae." Angie hung up. According to the clock on the wall, Mae's arrival would be cutting it close for the church's office hours. The rain outside eased enough to allow the morning light to penetrate into the alley along with the noise of a city fully awake. Every passing truck had her on edge. Her stomach growled loudly in the quiet office. "I can't believe how hungry I am."

"It is part of the healing." Sten pulled open a desk drawer, revealing a half-empty family-sized bag of M&Ms. "These smell edible."

"God, yes they are." She snatched up the bag and poured out a handful. "Want some?"

"I must admit I am curious. These are chocolate, correct?"

She raised a brow. "You've been on Earth how long, and you've never tasted chocolate?"

He shrugged and winced, his wing shuddering. "I have not been in a situation that provided the opportunity."

"Well, here." She grabbed his hand and filled it with the candies. "Eat up."

He tossed the handful into his mouth and his eyes went wide. His gaze went back to the bag in her hand.

"You like them."

"I can see why humans speak so highly of this food."

Laughing, she poured more into his hand. "Welcome to the dark side."

They finished the bag, then scouted the rest of the office for more food. Two ceramic coffee mugs sat on the edge of the desk, and Sten devoured one, but Angie stopped him when he reached for the one with World's Best Dad on it. "That probably means something to someone."

He nodded and withdrew his hand. Angie smiled tightly, trying not to think of all the memorabilia like that she was leaving behind. She should've asked Mae to grab something —anything—from her house. But then that might put her friend in greater danger than she was already in. Another truck rumbled past, and an airplane buzzed by overhead. Angie's gut clenched as she realized that meant Syndicate backup could arrive in the area at any time.

At ten minutes before ten, Angie took Sten's hand. The last thing they wanted was the pastor calling the cops because he discovered them inside. At least they might be able to pass off as Halloween partygoers outside. She shrugged into her damp robe, suppressing her urge to let her wings free as the terry-cloth rubbed against her shoulders. "We should wait out front for Mae."

As they exited the front doors, a skinny man was stepping out of a beaten-down Volvo parked along the sidewalk. He frowned at them, sizing up Sten's wings. "Can I help you?"

Angie's heart pounded frantically against her ribs. He must work here. They'd taken too long. Maybe she could beg sanctuary. Wasn't that a thing? "Are you the pastor here?"

"I am."

A semi rolled past, shaking the street. Behind it, Mae's truck appeared. Angie let out an explosive breath and grinned at the pastor. "Never mind. Our ride's here. Thank you."

Grabbing Sten's hand, she raced past the wide-eyed man toward Mae. Her friend gaped at them as Angie climbed into the passenger side. "You're the best, Mae."

Sten took one look at the cramped space, then catapulted into the bed, rocking the pickup. In the blink of an eye, he was lying flat against the bottom. "Drive," he commanded.

Mae's eyebrows were nearly at her hairline, but she put the truck into gear and pulled around the lumbering semi.

15

Angie watched through the pickup's rear glass in case anyone was following while Mae peppered her with questions. As far as she could tell, no one was following them—yet. But she didn't put it past the Syndicate to track them down. Her gaze kept drifting down to Sten lying flat in the back end, pelted by rain, his dislocated wing jouncing at every turn and bump. But until they were no longer surrounded by people, there was no other choice.

"Angie!" Mae's sharp tone finally jerked Angie's attention away from the window. "You're freaking me the hell out. What kind of shit have you gotten yourself into?"

"You wouldn't believe me." Angie rolled her shoulders and swallowed.

Mae shot a glance over her shoulder toward Sten. "Try me."

Letting out a long breath, Angie filled her friend in on everything. The sheriff's betrayal, the horrible fake FBI agents, even the baby.

"Back this truck up. You're pregnant?"

"I think so?" Her voice rose into a question on the last word and she let out a shaky laugh. "Can a doctor even tell if someone's pregnant that fast?"

"There are tests that can tell after seventy-two hours," Mae assured her. "But, damn, girl. I didn't realize you could get pregnant with a statue. Good thing that's never happened with my vibrator."

Leave it to Mae to break the tension. Angie huffed, the pressure in her chest easing slightly. "He's not a statue."

"I know." Mae winked at her. "Seriously, though, I wouldn't have guessed his DNA could even mix with a human's."

Angie cupped a hand over her belly. "I knew. I just didn't imagine it might happen so quickly."

Mae's brows drew together. "What do you mean?"

The pressure in Angie's chest returned, radiating toward her shoulders. *Keep it together, Angie.* Popping her wings inside the cab would probably make Mae crash. Swallowing down her instincts, Angie said, "I'm a hybrid. My whole family was part alien. That's why Sten's watched over us for so long."

A shaky breath escaped Mae, and she shook her head. "Girl, I always knew there was something special about you."

"You mean weird?" Angie couldn't help smiling.

"That, too. But really, who else do you know that can pull blackberry brambles with their bare hands?"

Angie thought about how many times people had commented on her lack of garden gloves. "You're right. I never thought about it before."

"I think you're the only person in town who hasn't come

into the clinic for one reason or another." Mae took the turn onto I-15. "By the way, I still don't know where we're going."

Glancing into the pickup bed, Angie met Sten's gaze and tried to smile. "Pull off at the next exit and let's find a back road where Sten can get out without attracting notice."

Mae looked Angie over. "What's with the bathrobe, anyway?"

"The sheriff arrested me this way."

"Seriously? What the hell? I shouldn't be surprised, though. Fucking sheriff." Mae shook her head and took the exit toward a no-name small town.

Reaching over, Angie squeezed Mae's arm. "By the way, thank you."

Mae nodded, keeping her eyes on the road. "You know I love you."

A silent sob convulsed Angie. "This is Area 51 stuff. They'll never stop chasing us. I can never go back home, Mae."

"After meeting Sten, I wondered if that might be what's going on." She pointed to a daypack on the floor of the passenger side. "I managed to swing by your house on the way here. Don't worry, I pretended I was there to pick you up for work. I brought you stuff."

Angie reached for the pack, wiping at her eyes with the back of her other hand. "You shouldn't have risked going there, but thank you." She glanced out the back window again, but the small town they were passing through didn't appear to have any other moving traffic. "I'll be relieved to have regular clothes."

Reaching inside, she found her favorite hoodie. Directly beneath that, she discovered the mason jar where she kept her heirloom seeds. She sucked in a breath, tears clouding her vision. "Mae!"

Her friend shot her a wry smile and turned onto a dirt road leading west into the mountains. "I figured of all the things you treasure, your garden is the most transportable."

Burying her face in her hands, Angie sobbed. She had no idea if her seeds would even grow on Sten's planet, but now she could at least try.

Mae's hand left the steering wheel to rub her back. The sensitive buds of Angie's wings responded by thrusting against the terry-cloth. Mae yelped and pulled back. "What is that?"

Angie sat up straight, grimacing against the cramping pain of her wings unable to unfurl beneath the robe. Mae'd been great about taking everything in stride, even the possibility of a half-alien baby. But how was she going to respond to wings? An old homestead with several junk cars in the overgrown yard rolled past outside. Ahead, the dirt road stretched into nothing but rolling sagebrush interspersed with a few pines and the snowcapped mountains beyond. Angie pointed to the side of the road. "Pull over here."

Mae slowed to a stop, the truck listing as the passenger side wheels rolled into the ditch. Her brown eyes kept looking between Angie's face and her shoulder. "Are those wings?"

"Hybrid, remember?" Angie whispered, shoulder blades aching with the effort of keeping her wings retracted.

Mouth dropping open, Mae reached over and jerked the neckline of Angie's robe aside. "No fucking way. Can you fly? Why didn't you ever tell me this? Show me!"

"Hold on, hold on!" Angie grappled with the robe, covering herself. "They're still new to me, so slow down."

Sten's face rose to fill the back window. "Are you injured?"

Angie's wings were straining against the robe, no matter how hard she concentrated on shoving them back inside. She yanked open the passenger side door and tumbled out, shedding her robe as she fell to her knees.

Mae cried, "Holy shit, that's awesome!" The sound of the truck door slamming and running feet. Then Mae was in front of her. "This really is Area 51 shit. You look like a naughty she-devil with wings in that lingerie. Can I touch one?"

"I… I guess." Angie smiled up at her, rising clumsily to her feet while her flapping wings tried to help.

Mae stepped back. "Whoa, watch the claws, woman."

"Sorry."

Sten leapt out of the truck bed and took her elbow. His touch was steadying in more ways than one.

Glancing back and forth between Angie and Sten, Mae shook her head. "Who would've thought my best friend's an alien. So where do you plan to hide?"

Sten's voice was a low rumble. "My people are sending a rescue ship at last. We must travel to the rendezvous point to meet it." He twisted to show Mae his injured wing. "But first, we must fix my wing."

Mae grimaced at the appendage. "Ouch. Looks dislocated." She cracked her knuckles. "I've set plenty of limbs, but never a wing. This is going to be interesting."

Within minutes and a few strained grunts, Sten's wing was set. Angie let out a sigh of relief, her own wings fluttering in empathy.

Sten retracted his into the slits in his back, resuming his more human shape. "Now you, *Hondassa*."

His encouragement helped, and Angie managed to withdraw her wings. She took a deep breath, glad to be back in her familiar form. The wings were going to take some getting used to.

Mae stepped around and began poking at her back. "Amazing how that works."

Sten raised his brows at Angie. She shrugged, letting Mae's fingers graze over her skin. "She's a doctor. She likes this stuff."

"Nurse Practitioner," Mae corrected automatically and finished her inspection. She came back around to face them, hands on her hips. "So, can you fly now?"

"Angie is not yet trained in flying." Sten's wings emerged once more. He flapped them, sending a gust of pine needles and dust rolling across the ground, and lifted a few feet. "I will carry us from here to the rendezvous point."

"How far away is that? I could just drive you." Mae reached over and took Angie's hand. "I wouldn't mind a few more hours together, since it sounds like I won't be seeing you again for a while."

Angie bit her lip, fighting back tears once more. She'd already cried more today than she had since her father's death. "I'd like that, Mae. Thank you."

Sten pulled his sigil from his pocket. "These coordinates indicate we must move that direction." He pointed north. "Approximately twelve hundred of your Earth miles."

Mae made a strangled noise. "I take it back. I can't drive you. Are there even roads that for north?"

"I do not know. Earthians call the location the Yukon Territory."

"Why can't the ship just pick us up here?" Angie asked.

Holy shit, she was planning on leaving on a space ship. *Well, you are an alien.* She flexed her shoulders, struggling to keep her rambunctious wings retracted.

Holding his sigil in one hand, Sten flicked through holographic screens of data. "Our sigils have a limited range for the teleportation device. Plus, the Prime Directive requires our fleet to remain as discreet as possible, even during a rescue mission. The location and time would have been selected due to a number of factors, most probably the scarcity of surveillance around the site." Sten closed his eyes and rubbed the base of one horn. "This journey will take us several days."

Mae's voice dropped to a whisper. "You're going to another planet. Will I ever talk to you again?"

Angie shook her head, ugly tears crumpling her face. "I don't know." The words ripped from her throat as she gripped Mae's hand. They stood like that for another long minute. "Will you take care of Sally and my house? My yellow climbing roses will die if they don't get watered once a week."

Mae swallowed, face creased and red, and choked out, "You know I have a black thumb, but I'll try not to kill anything." She stepped around Angie and reached into her purse for a pack of travel tissues. She blew her nose, then handed a tissue to Angie before rummaging once more in her purse. "Twelve hundred miles left on Earth. You're going to need money."

Angie stared at the bills. *Twelve hundred miles on Earth.* Such a long distance, and yet so short. How long would it take to fly there? "We can't take your money. You've already done too much."

"You're going to need to eat. Take it."

Reluctantly, Angie accepted the cash. Mae was right. Even now, Angie was ravenous. And Sten would need food to heal, as well. "Thank you."

"In fact, you'll need more than that if you have to travel more than a few days. Take my ATM card. Just stay away from caviar and casinos."

Suddenly, Angie remembered the gold stashed in her bed post. "I can pay you back." She told Mae how to find the coins. "Use whatever's left to take care of Sally and the house."

Mae grinned, but there was a sadness to her. "Tahiti, here I come."

Angie threw her arms around her friend. "I love you. Thank you for everything."

Mae hugged her back fiercely. "Call me if you can. Maybe that gold can pay for a collect call from another planet?"

"You're killing me," Angie said, swiping at stray tears. She'd miss Mae the most of anything. But her only chance at a future—the only future she wanted—was with Sten. She turned to him. "We need to go before I change my mind."

"There is no changing your mind. The Syndicate will track us down if we remain on Earth. If not us, then someday our child."

Without warning, Mae burst into loud tears. "I'm never gonna meet your rugrat!"

That set the waterworks off for Angie again. Sten waited patiently while the two hugged and Angie pulled on clothing. Then it was time. Strapping on the day pack, Angie stepped into Sten's arms. His hard chest and abs were a comfort as she watched Mae's waving form grow ever smaller until she was lost over the horizon.

16

Sten flew them over the sparsely wooded slopes at the base of the mountains, sticking to terrain that as yet remained inhospitable to mankind, carrying them ever north. When they came to roads or small towns, he'd rise into the clouds or at least high enough over the landscape that they'd be mistaken for a large bird by the casual observer. Angie clung to him, feeling like a baby orangutan, her shoulders itching inside her hoody. She was quite proud she'd been able to keep her wings retracted when they were screaming at her to open themselves to the wind.

An updraft thrust them upward, and her stomach lurched at the sudden motion. Once Sten had stabilized them, she asked, "Do you think I'll ever be able to fly?"

"Your wingspan seems sufficient to carry you at least for short distances. But for now, you must let me carry you."

But even Sten could not fly forever. They crossed the Canadian border while it was still light and stopped in a town called Cranston, choosing a motel that had doors that could be accessed from the parking lot. Angie checked in while Sten lurked outside. The moment she opened the door, he slipped inside and settled to the floor, his gray skin hardening. She was exhausted, and could hardly imagine how tired he must be after carrying her so many miles. And they still had so far to go. Her stomach rumbled; she had to find something to eat, soon.

She emptied her day pack and set out for the market she'd seen a few blocks north. Thanking Mae once more for the use of her ATM card, she filled the daypack with food. On the walk back, she devoured all six egg rolls she'd purchased at the deli, hoping Sten would forgive her for not bringing him one. Back at the hotel, he was still in *duramna,* so she sat in front of the TV and gorged herself on chips and chocolate cookies.

What kind of food would they have on Duras? Sten had been unfamiliar with chocolate, so no chocolate would suck. She licked the frosting from between the two halves of a cookie and let it melt on her tongue. Maybe she should stock up on chocolate to take with her.

She awoke to an infomercial on the TV. Sten still slept on the floor, hard as stone, so she rolled over and tried to sleep, but her mind was rolling a million miles a minute. She was leaving Earth. Leaving home. Everything had happened so fast. Literally days ago she'd been minding her own business and saving the seeds from her garden for next year. She'd always craved stability, always planned a life in Turnbull even when she'd gone away to college. Her father wanted better for her, but her heart was in Montana. Leaving it behind felt like a little piece of her soul had been excised.

Climbing out of bed, she turned the volume all the way

down and stretched out next to Sten, laying her head on his rocky shoulder. She should be cold, but she'd always been affected very little when it came to temperature extremes. She'd only seemed to become more impervious since the mating. Tough skinned, strong boned, temperature resistant, and now she had wings. Earth had been her home for twenty-seven years, but even her body was telling her she belonged on Duras.

She placed an open palm over Sten's chest where his heart must be beating. Did it beat while he was stone? She couldn't feel it.

Apparently sensing her restlessness, he shifted, reaching his other hand up to cover hers. "Can you not sleep, *Hondassa*?"

"I didn't mean to stop your healing. There's just a lot on my mind."

"I understand. Is there a way I can help?"

She pressed her lips against his hard chest, breathing in his earthy sweet scent. "Tell me about Duras."

He rolled to his side, drawing her against him. "It is a harsh planet, but beautiful, much the same as your high deserts on Earth, although our skies are violet rather than blue. But we lack resources. That was the reason my crew ended up crashing on your planet."

"You came to Earth looking for resources?" A sickness filled her stomach as she considered what this might mean for humanity.

"Not Earth." He stroked her hair. "We avoid planets with sentient life. Our mission was to explore the red planet you call Mars, but we were caught in a wormhole dilation that sent us out of control."

"So you've been away for a thousand years. What about your family back home? Do all of you live this long?"

"We do. And now, so will you."

She pulled back to get a better look at his face. "My father had more Khargal blood than I do, and he didn't live that long. He was ancient at a hundred and eight."

Sten smiled, his sharp canines catching the light flickering from the silent TV. "The *dassa* will extend your life to match mine."

Well, that was some shocking news. "So I'm going to live for what, a thousand years?"

"Or more. Our people often live well into their third millennia."

She let out a long breath, trying to imagine what she'd do with that much time. The trees she'd planted back on her property would be full grown by then. Not that she'd ever see them. "Do you think there's a chance we might ever come back to Earth?"

Sten took a long, slow breath. "I am not certain. But Earthians have come a long way in the time I have watched them. It is possible the planet will reach a stage at which my people will want to return and engage the inhabitants as equals."

She bit her lip, thinking about the way York and the other agent had talked about the "creatures." There were still people who believed some fellow humans were other; it could be a long time before Earth became enlightened enough to be approached by aliens as equals. Even if it did, by then it was likely everyone she knew and loved would be long gone. "I'm going to miss Earth."

"So will I," said Sten. "I have traveled with your family for many generations and seen much of your planet."

Angie realized how little she'd seen of her own world. Would she regret never having taken the opportunity to travel? "Tell me more."

They spent the rest of the night talking about her ancestors, the trials they'd endured as they moved across continents over the generations. Angie'd been so tied up in her one tiny plot of land, she'd never realized just how far her heritage actually stretched. *Beyond Earth, even.*

Perhaps she really was about to go home.

ith a few weeks until the ship arrived at the rendezvous location, Sten took his time, allowing Angie to enjoy her last bit of time on her home planet. She didn't mind the shoddy hotel rooms as long as she was with Sten. But after exploring the first couple of small towns on her own, Angie decided she didn't much care for travel. She was looking forward to settling down again. But she did savor playing on pristine snowy slopes, making love beneath the starry night sky, bathing in hidden hot springs, and gorging on chocolate. She even got to practice using her wings a little, jumping from the sharp peaks of mountains and gliding to a stop at the snowy base.

They'd reached the rendezvous site a few days ago and discovered a number of cabins that were vacant this late in the season. Each morning, they checked the sigil's interface, watching the white dots marking the locations of the other sigils converge toward the mountain. She'd asked him if he wanted to meet up with those nearby, but he'd only shaken his head and said there would be time enough for that. He wanted her all to himself.

Early on the morning of the rendezvous, Angie stood on the stony outcropping near their cabin, overlooking a gorgeous blue-green river. She shrugged off her parka and spread her wings, letting out a frosty sigh. The moon stood out like a pale disk in the morning sky, and the weak sun had begun melting the frost from the nearby trees.

Sten moved up behind her and took her hand, speaking around a mouthful of breakfast candy. "I am going to miss this Earthian food."

"I've got more in our pack." She'd stuffed every spare inch of her duffel bag with Sten's new favorite food, although she couldn't seem to stomach chocolate for breakfast, either due to pregnancy or just nerves about leaving. "But if you keep eating it at this rate, none will ever make it back to Duras."

"We may be able to convince my people to begin negotiations with Earth sooner than expected if they learn of this delicacy."

"Well, if someone could get their hands on some viable cocoa beans, I might be able to grow it."

Sten's eyes widened. "This comes from a plant?"

"Yep." She smirked. How fun would it be to grow chocolate? But then, she'd also have to figure out how to harvest and process it. And they'd need sugar...

The sun cleared the mountain and hit the blue-green thread of open water below, dazzling her with its brilliance. Angie pulled her hand free of his. "Let's fly."

She leapt off the outcrop over the river, holding her wings

steady as they bore her weight through the frigid wind. She wasn't very strong yet so could only go a short distance, plus she couldn't fly in her parka, but she didn't seem to get as cold as someone else would in this weather; the short flight over the majestic scenery was definitely worth a few goose-bumps and sore muscles.

The swoosh of Sten's wings came from behind her, and she looked over her shoulder at him, grinning. She loved the freedom she felt in the air. But she was also grateful for Sten's watchful presence. More than once, he'd caught her before her strength gave out and sent her crashing to the ground. He said fledglings crashed a lot and suffered broken bones all the time, hence the Khargal ability for accelerated healing. But he didn't want his *Hondassa* to suffer through that.

Banking left she followed the river toward an area of rapids, the frothing water frozen into amazing arcs and swirls. Far below, a moose and her calf strode through knee-deep snow, nibbling the tips of branches. In the distance, the beat of a helicopter pounded the air, and Angie dropped, afraid she might be seen.

Sten's arms caught her, bearing her gently to the powdery snow. She snuggled up against him, trying to gather some warmth. His voice rumbled through her. "I believe the others are congregating on the peak. We should get our things."

Angie retracted her wings and Sten encircled her in his arms to fly her back to the cabin. Retrieving her parka from the ledge where she'd dropped it, she went inside and retrieved the duffel and the daypack, checking around to be sure they weren't forgetting anything. It felt strange to be saying goodbye to a rustic cabin rather than her house. She'd shed many tears about leaving, but also felt ready to embrace a new life like her adventurous forefathers. A new life with Sten.

She shrugged into their daypack and looped the duffel over an arm, then walked from the cabin, shutting the door firmly behind her. Sten already waited on the ledge, looking out toward the peak. He put an arm around her and pulled her close. "Ready?"

She nodded.

Bunching his muscles, he launched above the trees. Across the horizon she spotted what could only be another Khargal taking to the air and heading toward the mountain's peak. She gulped against the frigid wind as he sped toward a ledge on the mountain, tears streaming from her eyes. The higher they went, the colder it became, until her fingers were numbly clutching his neck. "How high do we need to be for the teleport?"

"This should be far enough." Sten set her down on a rocky outcropping a short way above the tree line. The wind blew so hard, the snow couldn't stick to the ledge, and she cringed against Sten just to keep herself from being blown off. Squinting over the curve of the earth, she caught a glimpse of yet another Khargal rising toward the mountain. The sun glittered in the fine mist of snow blowing past her, as if she was surrounded by diamonds. She put a mittened hand to her throat where the sigil hung. "How do we know they can see us? I'm a little nervous about being teleported."

"Don't worry, they know we are here. The teleportation can be disconcerting at first." Sten angled one wing to shelter her from the wind. "But I will be right there with you."

The crystals of snow grew brighter, developing an almost golden hue. A tingle spread through her limbs.

The next thing she knew, she was retching on her hands and knees. Her wings were on fire. She reared back, grappling at her shoulders, finding the straps of the daypack. Then the vomiting overtook her again, flinging her to her knees.

Several sets of clawed feet surrounded her, and someone spoke a guttural language overhead. She twisted her head to gape up at three Khargals in form-fitting blue and gray suits. Saying something she couldn't understand, one reached a hand toward her, razor-sharp claws fully extended.

She jerked back. "Sten!" More pain lanced through her and she screamed.

And then the world went black.

☙❦❧

When she awoke, the strangers were gone and Sten was brushing his lips against hers. "*Hondassa*, wake up."

Behind him, pale curved walls gave off a sort of ambient light, and a strangely earthy scent that was both familiar and foreign assaulted her nose, making her stomach grow queasy again. Her chest felt tight, and she glanced down at her breasts to see her torso thickly encased in some sort of clear film. "Where am I?"

"In our cabin. Your wings are broken." His brow ridges were pinched into a concerned line.

"Broken?" She tried to remember the teleportation, but that only made her stomach churn again. "How'd that happen?"

"You extended your wings when you emerged from the teleport. I should have realized that might happen. It is a common response to stress. Your daypack and parka were in the way, and during your thrashing, you snapped several bones."

A shiver ran through her. The entire event was hazy. But she did remember one thing. "One of those other Khargals tried to slash me."

Sten shook his head. "He was trying to cut you free of the daypack." Touching a spot behind her ear, he said, "You now have a translation ship so you will not mistake a crewman's words again."

She raised her brows, following where he'd touched behind her ear. A minuscule raised bump was the only indication something was there. "You mean I don't need to learn to speak Khargal?"

He shook his head. "Duras is home to many different species. We find the use of a translation device the most expedient way to handle language barriers."

"Is that how you know English?"

"Unfortunately not. We had not met Earthians prior to our crash, so had to learn Earth's various dialects the hard way. But now that several of us are fluent, all of Earth's languages will be added to our translation database."

"Handy." She rolled to her side and pushed herself to sit. Her hands and legs were free, but her back and chest were encased in what felt like a flexible cast of some sort. She tried to look over her shoulder but couldn't see. "So, are my wings going to be okay?"

"The doctor believes so. He was not comfortable enough with human physiology to administer a healing serum, so I'm afraid you'll have to bear with the cast for a while yet."

"My mouth tastes like crap." She glanced around for a

glass of water. The room was strangely organic, with honeycomb pockets in the walls and curves instead of corners. Definitely nothing human. The bed seemed to be almost an afterthought.

Sten leaned down and retrieved a cup with a straw. "Here."

She sipped lightly, surprised by the lightly flavored beverage. "What is this?"

"An herbal tea my people find helpful during pregnancy."

She finished it and handed the cup back to him. Her head felt stuffed with cotton, and the ache between her shoulder blades pulsed in time with her heartbeat, but she felt much better than she had coming off the teleport. Then what he'd said hit her. "Pregnancy. Did the doctor verify it?"

Sten took her hand and pressed a kiss into her palm, his emerald eyes soft. "Indeed. I never dreamed of being happier than this."

Her heart melted. "I love you Sten." As she said it, she realized that although they'd mated, she'd never spoken those words. She felt them now to the very core of her being.

"I love you, too, my *Hondassa*." He lowered his face to hers and kissed her softly. "You might also be happy to know we have taken other humans on board. It seems I am not the only Khargal to have taken a human mate."

A warmth spread through her as she realized she wasn't going to be the only human on Duras after all.

EPILOGUE

Sten rubbed home-made sunscreen over his infant son's horn buds, smiling down into the chubby, pink face. The harsh sun of Duras was not kind to some hybrid's skin, but Angie had come up with a botanical emollient for herself and other humans who needed it. In fact, her whole garden had become a haven for Earthians who wanted a taste of their home world now and again. She'd even begun negotiations with the Khargal military to sponsor a horticultural excursion back to Earth so she could acquire more seeds.

The baby cooed and kicked, tail circling Sten's wrist. "Hold still, William." The human name still felt strange on his tongue. Sten wiped the rest of the sunscreen across the bridge of the fledgling's nose. "Let us go see what your dame and your brother are doing."

Outside the ground-level home, a lush oasis of greenery spread across the rocky ground. Angie's water conservation techniques and her drought-resistant Earth plants had attracted a lot of attention, and she'd even been granted a waiver to double her water allotment in order to expand the gardens. She really wanted to add a water garden, but had not managed to get that approved.

He carried the baby between the leaves, keeping to the shady paths Angie had created. Ahead, he heard little Graj chattering at his mother and Angie's soft responses. Following the sound, he emerged on a newly tilled section of ground to find his oldest son and *Hondassa* crouched on either side of a tiny seedling.

Graj held a clod of soil in one hand, his tiny wings not yet functional but fluttering behind him as if trying to take off on their own. Sten smiled with pride at the youngling's three small horns; Angie's Khargal bloodline was strong to produce a son with more horns than his sire. William's buds were just beginning to show, but Sten had already counted three there, as well.

Angie glanced up, smiling as Sten entered the clearing. "Graj has a green thumb just like his momma."

"I bet." He handed William a fist-sized rock to suck on and set him into the wheeled pen Angie called a crib.

Graj abandoned his clod of dirt and ran over to play with his little brother.

Angie dusted her hands off on the front of her pants and moved toward Sten, her wings fanning against her back. Her cheeks were pink, and he smoothed his fingertips over them, hoping any residual sunscreen might transfer to her skin. "You have tours scheduled today?"

The garden attracted so much notice, Angie had begun scheduling regular times for visitors to show up, otherwise she was running outside to show people around at all hours of the day and sometimes night. She gave him a wicked grin.

"Not a single one. Your mother's coming by to take the kids until tomorrow night."

"Ah, you have plans, do you?" He wrapped both arms around her middle and pulled her close. "Do they involve me?"

"All my plans include you, my love." She lifted her face and grazed his chin with a playful bite. He shivered. He loved it when she did that. He lowered his mouth against hers and gave her a languid kiss, breathing in her Earthian essence, a perfume of plants and stone that was purely Angie.

She tightened her arms around his waist and kissed him back, her lips giving him promises of what would come later. When they let up, she glanced over her shoulder to check on Graj and William, then pulled away to reach for a shovel. "But until she gets here, I need your help."

"Slave driver." He grinned at her. "But I'm always happy to be a part of your garden."

Her smile was enough to melt a stone man's heart.

THE END

D ear Reader,

Did you enjoy Sten and Angie's story? Not ready to leave the Khargal world? Then check out Etched in Stone by Abigail Myst. Or if you've finished the series, you can start a new one with dangerous alien pirates, strong women, and awesome world-building in Galactic Pirate Brides!

Start your adventure with Rescued by Qaiyaan, where a clever female ex-con is about to rock this hot alien captain's world. Keep reading for a Sneak Peek!

Until next time, keep your eye on the skies!
Tamsin

P.S. If you enjoyed reading this story, it would mean a lot to me if you would leave a quick review. Indie authors like myself rely on your word of mouth in this tough publishing world! Thank you!

GLOSSARY

At-Ukris: aerial Duras animal. Looks like a cross between an eagle and an octopus roughly the size of a whale

Bansial: the Durassian word for sticky

Canikin: the Durassian word for lady parts

Dam: mother

Dassa: mating fluid

Duramna: stone form

Duras: Khargal home planet

Durassian: the Khargal language

Earthian: what Khargals call humans

Fa: the Durassian word for Mrs.

Grack: the Durassian expletive for fuck

Guurlk: Khargal liquor

Hondassa: Mate

Kher: Khargal term for siblings

Khargal: what gargoyles call themselves

Lar: the Durassian word for god

Macero: the Durassian expletive for hell

Maztek: Duras animal similar to an earth whale

Rose Syndicate: clandestine organization that is pursuing gargoyles and their technology

Sartek: a random predatory animal on Duras

Sigil: the device used for contacting the rescue beacon and teleporting to the rescue ship

Sire: father

Tanem: the Durassian word for temporary companion taken before a true mate

Want more sexy Khargals? Check out all the books in the series! You don't want to miss a single one!

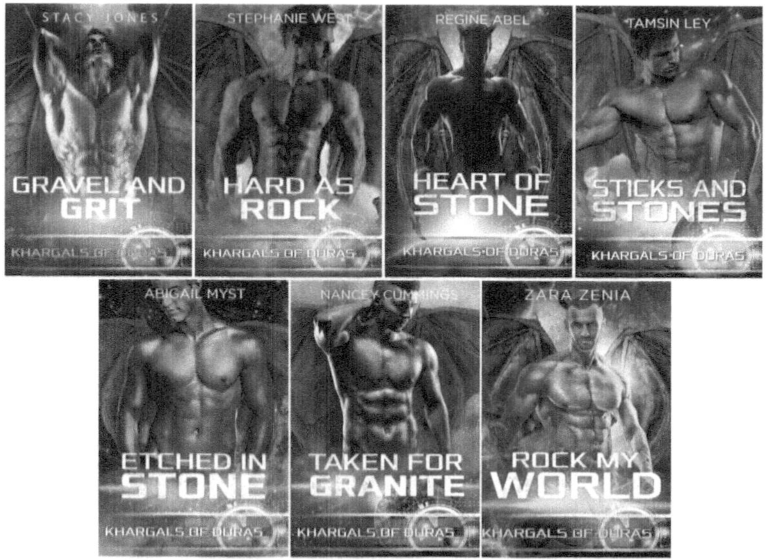

https://nanceycummings.com/khargals-of-duras/

SNEAK PEEK OF RESCUED BY QAIYAAN

"I recognize your ship, Captain Qaiyaan." The voice coming over the ship's comm deepened with menace. "You're interfering with a legal salvage operation."

The two ships rotating helplessly outside Qaiyaan's port screen told a different story than the human on the comm was telling; an eyeful of stars peeked through the blackened hole piercing the Syndicorp passenger ship's hull, while the second, unmarked vessel's short-range lasers glowed from recent use. "Seems you ought to be a bit more generous," Qaiyaan drawled. "What with needing our help and all. I'm gonna take first crack at the salvage, then we'll get you your part. You can have whatever we leave behind."

"I warn you, don't touch that ship!" blustered the voice on the other end.

Normally Qaiyaan'd wish the other pirate captain well and move on. Not today. His crew hadn't had a profitable job in half a Denaidan year. This opportunity was too good to pass up. Besides, anyone who blew a hole in an unarmed passenger transport—Syndicorp or otherwise—left a sour taste in Qaiyaan's mouth. "I could simply wait here. My first mate estimated in half a day we'll have two ships in need of salvage. This is an awful deep part of space to find yourselves without a spare flux modulator."

"You fucking son-of-a-rakwiji-whore bastard! I have powerful friends, and I can make sure you never find safe harbor in this sector again!"

Qaiyaan crossed his arms and glared at the comm. "I'm the *only* friend you have in the galaxy at this moment, so I suggest you be polite."

Noatak, Qaiyaan's first mate, grinned at him from the navigator's seat, the copper sheen of his skin reflecting the multi-colored light from the control panels. The small cockpit, designed for humans, was barely big enough for the two Denaidan males to breathe at the same time. "Want me to take us in for soft docking?"

Qaiyaan watched the human pirate ship complete another slow, helpless turn in the port monitor. "Take us in, but keep an eye out for anything suspicious. Could be a Syndicorp trap."

"Pretty elaborate for a setup." Noatak shook his head, the metal beads decorating his long hair and beard clicking softly.

"Chances of blowing both in-line flux modulators at once *and* not having a spare? Either he's stupid, or it's a setup."

"I say he's stupid." Noatak adjusted the controls to nose the *Hardship* toward the passenger wreckage.

Qaiyaan rose from the captain's chair. Shit happened, especially to ships running less-than-legal activities. He ought to know, having just forked out the proceeds from their latest heist to retrofit a new hull onto the *Hardship's* battle-damaged frame. The black market repairman'd all but asked Qaiyaan to bend over and spread his cheeks. Rotten, cheating bastard.

Turning to the door, he paused and looked over his shoulder at Noatak. "Just be careful. Even if it's not a trap, Syndicorp'll be looking for their missing ship, and I don't want to be caught with our dicks out."

After sealing the control room door, he slid down the ladder to the cargo bay, booted feet clanging against the catwalk grating as he landed. "Mekoryuk! Tovik! All hands on deck!"

Mekoryuk poked his clean-shaven face out of the med bay. He was the only crew member who chose not to wear the customary full beard the Denaida prided themselves on, citing a doctor's need for cleanliness or some such *anaq*. "What is it?"

"Salvage mission. Assume zero atmo. No time for suits. Syndicorp could be riding our ass any minute. Where's Tovik?"

"Where else?" Mek tilted his head toward the end of the hall.

Qaiyaan left the doctor and strode to where the hatch to the engine room stood open. As captain, he could appreciate the well-oiled hum of a ship's engines, but Tovik was a bit too much in love with moving parts. Squatting next to the hole, Qaiyaan yelled, "Tovik! On deck ready for void! And bring a spare in-line flux modulator! Now!"

Knowing his crewmen would comply without further prodding, he headed for the airlock. Through the portal, he watched Noatak guide the magnetic grappler into place. The captain of the human ship was probably apoplectic, watching his cash cow get raped by another ship. *Tough luck.* Qaiyaan'd be sure to leave the replacement flux modulator within reach, but not until the *Hardship* was ready to hightail it out of there.

The first mate finessed the grappler toward the other ship's open airlock, his voice crackling over the internal comm to the cargo bay. "You sure you don't want to take time to suit up?"

Mekoryuk arrived with a med-kit over his shoulder, and Qaiyaan shot him a grin as he answered. "No suits. These *qumli* need the practice."

Tovik pounded up, feet bare as usual, his scruffy beard and hair not quite the full mane of a mature Denaida male. Qaiyaan scowled at him, looking pointedly at his gleaming copper feet. The youngster said he had better control of his ionic abilities if his skin was bare, but one of these days he was going to lose a toe, or worse. At least the boy carried the spare flux modulator, as requested.

While Noatak secured the flexi-tube between the ships, Qaiyaan filled in the other crew members. "I'm not sure what we'll find over there, but it's not likely to be pretty. Grab everything not nailed down. We'll sort our inventories later."

Mek asked, "What about survivors?"

"There's no life signs aboard." Qaiyaan pointed to the modulator in Tovik's hands. "That'll stay with the human ship once we leave. Can you give it a slow push their direction? I don't want it to reach them until we're long gone."

"You bet, Captain!" the young man nodded, likely already calculating trajectory and speed at which to push the thing.

"Stand fast for void!" Noatak's voice echoed through the cargo bay.

Qaiyaan barely had time to summon his ionic shell before the doors cracked open. A blast of air swept past, rattling the flexi-tube as it sucked into the other ship and out the gaping hole in its hull. The Denaidan's ability to withstand vacuum had made them one of the most sought-after races for Syndicorp marine crews before the catastrophe had ended their world. Now…

Now they were just pirates.

Concentrating on keeping his feet on the deck, Qaiyaan tapped his temple to activate his cochlear implant. A vestige of his days as a trooper, it came in handy in zero atmo when they couldn't bother with suits and the attached comms.

The three crewmen pushed themselves along the flexi-tube into the darkness of the other ship. Tovik, ever prepared, pulled a floodlight from his belt and slapped it to the inner wall of the passenger ship. The illumination exposed a passenger cabin surprisingly gutted of anything passenger-related. No nav-grav seats for humanoids, no methane tanks for garan'uks, not even any acceleration webbing for yanipa-nimayu. Instead, cargo containers of all shapes and sizes floated freely within the cabin, some cracked open and spilling their contents in haloes around them.

What the hell is this ship? Qaiyaan wondered. He'd been expecting the gruesome sight of space-bloated passengers. Not that he minded this alternative. He reached out and grabbed a floating package of hypodermic needles. *Medical supplies?*

He exchanged a glance with Tovik, who shrugged. Whatever this stuff was didn't matter; he'd much rather deal with salable goods than corpses.

Qaiyaan pushed toward the nearest container until he could get a hand on it and shoved the man-sized box toward the flexi-tube, relying on inertia to carry it most of the way.

One after another, he moved containers, working until sweat coated his skin beneath his ionic shielding. Even in zero-G, it took effort to hold himself steady and force the heavy boxes into motion. At least twenty minutes passed before he grew light-headed. Using the ionic shell was much like a diver holding his breath, and he knew they'd soon have to come up for air. A tinny voice in his implant did the job for him. "We have incoming on long-range, Captain. Can't yet tell if it's Syndicorp, but they'll be in range for ID in eight minutes."

Anaq. They'd come looking faster than he'd expected. He raised his arm and caught the other men's attention, circling two index fingers overhead to tell them to wrap it up. The men dropped what they were doing and moved toward the exit.

As soon as the door sealed, blessed oxygen began to fill the bay, but it would be a few minutes before there was enough pressure to breathe. Still light-headed, Qaiyaan began helping secure the containers against the floor's mag-locks. He estimated they'd emptied at least half the salvage and was feeling quite pleased as Noatak began accelerating away from the derelict ship.

"Captain?" Mek called from behind a stack of containers.

At that same moment, Noatak's voice crackled through the bay's comm. "Confirmed Syndicorp ship closing in fast. We need to burn, ASAP."

"We need five minutes," Qaiyaan said, assessing the remaining cargo.

"Captain!" Mekoryuk called again. "We have a problem."

"What?" Qaiyaan leaned around the corner. Tovik and the medic stood over a cargo box, staring down at a portal in its surface. Blinking red light bounced off both their faces.

Tovik rubbed his hand vigorously across the small window. "Is that a girl?"

"You've got to be fucking kidding me." Qaiyaan slapped a mag clamp against the container he was securing and stood. "A cryo-pod? Who the hell picked that up?"

"You said grab everything," Tovik said. He looked up to meet Qaiyaan's gaze. "Can we keep her?"

Noatak came over the com again. "Captain, they're hailing us."

Qaiyaan scowled and thrust a finger at the cryo-pod. "She's not a *netorpuk* puppy, Tovik. Just secure the damn thing so we can burn. We'll figure out what to do with it later."

"That's the problem," Mek said. "The cryo's failing. She won't survive a burn in this state."

"Fuuuck." Qaiyaan stomped over to the pod. He should have known things were going too easy. Looking at the face through the glass, his mouth grew suddenly dry. A young woman with long charcoal hair lay inside, a crescent of dark lashes against her high cheekbones. The blinking red light near her head illuminated her perfectly sculpted features as if coating them with blood.

"Just vent it," Noatak spoke over the line. "Let Syndicorp pick it up."

Tovik grabbed the end as if claiming the pod as his own. "You can't do that. What if they miss her?"

Noatak answered, "Not our problem."

"You should see what she looks like…" Tovik continued.

Now wasn't the time to argue over crew shares of the spoils, but Qaiyaan felt a sudden desire to wrestle the pod away from his engineer and claim the contents for himself. He tamped down the feeling. If they didn't get moving immediately, Syndicorp troopers would shoot first and ask questions later.

Noatak's voice boomed over his thoughts. "*Anaq*! They just obliterated the human ship!"

Syndicorp is out for blood today. Clenching his jaw, Qaiyaan shoved Tovik aside and began pushing the box toward the airlock, averting his gaze from the breath-taking face inside. "If we vent her, they'll have to stop and pick her up, which'll give us more time to get away."

"But, Captain—" Tovik started.

"We're not murderers!" Mek shouted, moving to intercept the box.

The comm filled the bay again. "Captain, you're not going to like this." Noatak's voice had gone from excited panic to deadly quiet. Qaiyaan ceased pushing, turning to face the speaker as if he could read his first mate's face from here. Noatak only used that voice when something deadly was going on. "They took out the passenger ship, too. There's nothing left of either vessel but a haze of space dust."

The breath left Qaiyaan's body. Syndicorp'd destroyed their own ship? Why would they do that?

Mek moved close to the captain, his voice low. "Venting her is a death sentence."

Qaiyaan squeezed his eyes shut. Why could nothing ever be easy? This woman was probably some scrawny human female on an exorbitant corporate cryo-vacation or some such nonsense. But he couldn't just leave her, not to the mercy of space, and definitely not to a ship that was blowing up everything in its path. "How long do you need to wake her?"

"The waking cycle takes twenty minutes."

He leveled a glare at the medic. "I didn't ask how long it takes. I asked how long you need."

Mek shook his head. "I can pull her out now, but she'll take days to recuperate. And she'll still be too weak to strap in for burn."

"Days to recuperate is better than minutes to end up as space dust. Pull her. We can link our ionic shells to protect her during burn."

Mek's right eye twitched. "We're exhausted from scavenging in zero atmo. I'm not sure we can withstand the strain."

"Do you have a better suggestion? If you do, make it now, because we're out of time."

"They'll be in range in thirty seconds, Captain," Noatak clipped out, his voice still deadly steady.

Mek's jaw bulged, but he nodded. "Fine. I think I've got enough stims to keep us up and running afterward. But let's not make a habit of it."

Popping the pod's seals, Qaiyaan knelt to lift the frigid human from the padded interior. She was naked, her nipples peaked from the cold. His hand slid beneath her nicely rounded bottom, every ionic sensor in his skin aware of the contact. He tried to remain focused on her face instead of the silky smooth curve of her hip cradled against his chest. Her eyes fluttered but didn't open.

Laying her on the deck, he stretched out beside her, grounding himself to the metal decking. Enveloping her in his power. Locking his body against hers.

Tovik sat cross-legged at her head, his bare feet tucked beneath him, and placed both his hands on her shoulders. But his gaze was on her upright nipples. Come to think of it,

Qaiyaan's were, too, so he couldn't blame the young engineer. Mek spread out along her other side. An unfamiliar twinge made Qaiyaan want to shove them both away.

Hoping he hadn't just given all four of them a death sentence, Qaiyaan called out, "Engage full burn."

Ready to keep reading? Get your copy now!

ACKNOWLEDGMENTS

Collaborating on this series was a challenging experience for me, and I learned so much. I want to thank my Jitters Critters and my beta readers for their quick and thoughtful comments, my husband for being so supportive during my endless eighty-hour work weeks, and my daughter for forcing me to leave the computer and take a quick walk around the block with her. :)

I also want to thank the other authors in this series—my GarGals—for their endless patience and tough skins. We all had strengths contributing to this venture, and I know we all shed tears at some point in the process. I want to thank each and every one of you for your efforts to make this series a success. I am proud to call you not only my colleagues, but also my friends.

ABOUT THE AUTHOR

Once upon a time I thought I wanted to be a biomedical engineer, but experimenting on lab rats doesn't always lead to happy endings. Now I blend my nerdy infatuation of science with character-driven romance and guaranteed happily-ever-afters. My monsters always find their mates, with feisty heroines, tortured heroes, and all the steamy trouble they can handle. I promise my stories will never leave you hanging (although you may still crave more!)

When I'm not writing, I'll be in the garden or the kitchen, exploring Alaska with my husband, or preparing for the zombie apocalypse. I also love wine and hard apple cider, am mediocre at crochet, and have the cutest 12-pound bunny named Abigail.

Interested in more about me? Join my VIP Club and get free books, notices, and other cool stuff!

www.mates4monsters.com